"There's something I want to show you."

Dan indicated an old-fashioned telescope set on a stand near the window. It looked across the bay of the lake. Julie adjusted it to her eyes, and then made an unexpected discovery.

"Those lights shining there—that's my hotel, isn't it?" she said with surprise. "And if it was daytime...."

"You could see the cove below..." Dan finished with amusement.

Julie gasped. "You mean you saw me? You trained that telescope on me? But... but I could have been doing anything," she objected.

"Like swimming in the raw?" He smiled.

"And you came to find me?" Julie asked.

"I tried for days," he said. "That coastline has dozens of inlets. I didn't even know about the hotel until someone told me. But I've found you now and I won't let you go!"

Other titles by

ANNE MATHER
IN HARLEQUIN PRESENTS

Other titles by

ANNE MATHER
IN HARLEQUIN ROMANCES

Many of these titles, and other titles in the Harlequin Romance series, are available at your local bookseller. For a free catalogue listing all available Harlequin Presents and Harlequin Romances, send your name and address to:

HARLEQUIN READER SERVICE,
M.P.O. Box 707,
Niagara Falls, N.Y. 14302
Canadian address:
Stratford, Ontario, Canada N5A 6W2

ANNE MATHER

spirit of atlantis

Harlequin Books

TORONTO · LONDON · NEW YORK · AMSTERDAM
SYDNEY · HAMBURG · PARIS · STOCKHOLM

Harlequin Presents edition published April 1980
ISBN 0-373-10351-4

Original hardcover edition published in 1980
by Mills & Boon Limited

CHAPTER ONE

JULIE made her way down through the trees, her sandalled feet sliding on the needled slope. The smell of pine and juniper was all around her, mingling with the earthy scents of the forest, and although there were occasional scufflings in the underbrush, she was no longer alarmed. After making this particular descent every morning since her arrival, she was used to the shy retreat of the small animals that lived in these woods, and she had no real fear of meeting any human intruder. Pam and David's cabin-style hotel was situated way off the beaten path, and she doubted any intrepid motorist would risk the forest track. Their visitors came by yacht or canoe or motor boat, and just occasionally on foot, but as no one new had arrived within the last couple of days, Julie felt safe in assuming she would not be disturbed.

At this hour of the morning, and it was only a little after six o'clock, the lake held no appeal for their predominantly middle-aged clientele, and Julie had grown accustomed to considering it her private time of the day. Soon enough, the vast reaches of Lake Huron would be invaded by speedboats towing sun-bronzed water-skiers, and paddle steamers giving their passengers a glimpse of some of the thirty thousand islands for which the lake was famous. But right now, it was quiet, as quiet as in the winter, when the lake was frozen over to a depth of several feet. Then, the animals had it all their own way, and the summer settlers returned to their centrally-heated homes, and dreamed about the long sunny days at the lake.

Georgian Bay—even the names had a special sound, Julie thought. Beausoleil Island, Waubanoka, Penetang Rock, the

5

Giant's Tomb—she had visited them all in the three weeks since her arrival, and she loved their natural beauty and the timeless sense of space. She was grateful to Adam for giving her these weeks, weeks to recover from the terrible shock of her father's suicide, and she was grateful to the Galloways, too, for making this holiday possible.

She heard the splashing in the water long before she reached the rocky shoreline. It wasn't the usual sucking sound the water made as it fell back from splashing against the numerous rocks, but a definite cleaving of the lake's surface, followed by a corresponding insurge of rippling waves right to the edge of the incline.

Julie frowned as she emerged from the trees and saw the dark head in the water. She had half suspected it, of course, and yet she was still disappointed, the more so when she saw the heap of clothes lying on the rocks at her feet. They looked like a man's clothes, but these days who could be sure? Jeans were asexual, and the denim shirt could have belonged to anyone.

Her brain flicked swiftly through a mental catalogue of the guests at present staying at the hotel. Perhaps it was one of them, and yet none of them seemed the type to take an early morning dip. There were the Fairleys, but he was fat and middle-aged, and unlikely to shed his clothes in anything less than a sauna, and she was simply not the type. The Meades? Again she dismissed the idea. They were much younger, but they seldom appeared before noon, and Pam had already speculated on their being a honeymoon couple. So who? Only the Edens were left, and a Mrs and Miss Peters, but she couldn't imagine Richard Eden being allowed to go anywhere without his wife and their two whining children, and neither Geraldine Peters nor her mother would wear anything so inelegant as jeans.

A feeling of intense irritation gripped her. This man, and she was pretty sure he was male, had ruined her day, and she felt vaguely resentful. She was in the annoying position of not knowing what she ought to do, and while it would obviously be simpler to turn and go back to her cabin, she didn't see why she should behave as if she didn't have the right to be there. She probably had more right than he had, even if no one had troubled to put up signs saying it was private land.

She was still standing there, gazing rather morosely in his direction, when he turned and saw her. There was no mistaking his sudden reaction, or the fact that he was now swimming strongly towards her. It made her unaccountably nervous, but she stood her ground as he got nearer. It was only as he got near enough for her to see his face that she realised his appraisal was coolly insolent, and her denim shorts seemed unsuitable apparel for someone who wanted to appear distant.

'Hi!'

To her astonishment she realised he was addressing her, and indignation at his audacity made her gulp a sudden intake of breath. He was obviously under the delusion that she had been watching him out of curiosity, and perhaps he thought she was interested in him.

Ignoring him, she deliberately turned her head, shading her eyes, and making a display of gazing out across the water. Perhaps if she showed him she wasn't interested, he would take his clothes and go away, and she could enjoy the solitary swim she had looked forward to.

'Hi—*you*!'

The masculine tones were faintly mocking now, the familiar salutation suffixed by an equally annoying pronoun. Just who did he think he was? she thought indignantly, and turned glacial green eyes in his direction.

He was treading water a few feet from the shore, making no apparent effort to get out. The lake bed shelved quite rapidly, and he was still out of his depth, but she could see how brown his skin was, and how long the slick wet hair that clung below his nape.

'Will you please stop bothering me?' she exclaimed, un-happily aware that the skimpy halter bra of her bikini was hardly the kind of attire to afford any degree of dignity, and his crooked grin seemed to echo her uneasy suspicions.

'Those are my clothes on the rock beside you,' he called, and she was momentarily struck by the familiarity of his accent. Was he English? Was it possible to meet another English person in this very Canadian neck of the woods, or was it simply his accent didn't match that of the Gallo-ways or any of the other residents staying at the hotel? Whatever, she quickly disposed of her curiosity, and in her most frigid tones, she retorted:

'I can see that. Now will you please put them on and get out of here?'

'I will—put them on, I mean, if you'll be a good girl and go away,' he replied, allowing his mocking gaze to move over her in admiring appraisal. 'Unless you'd like to join me?'

'No, thank you.' Julie was not amused by his invitation. 'And why should *I* go away? This land belongs to the Kawana Point Hotel. You're trespassing!'

'The lake belongs to everyone,' he retorted, pushing back his hair with long fingers. 'Now will you let me get out of here? It's pretty damn cold.'

'I'm not stopping you,' Julie responded coldly, flicking the towel she carried against her legs. 'And no one asked you to swim.'

'No, they surely didn't,' he agreed, his accent sounding distinctly southern at that moment. 'But I don't have no swimsuit, little lady, so unless you have no objections——'

Julie turned away before he had finished speaking, her features burning with indignant colour. How dare he go swimming without a pair of trunks? It was disgusting, it was *indecent*!

'Okay, you can look now.'

The mocking voice was nevertheless disturbing, and she

glanced round half apprehensively to find he had put on the denim jeans and was presently shouldering his way into the matching shirt. He had obviously not brought a towel either, and the pants clung in places Julie would rather not look, emphasising his lean hips and the powerful muscles of his thighs. He was tall, easily six feet, with a lean but not angular build, and he carried his height easily, moving with a lithe and supple fluidity as he crossed the rocks towards her.

Julie took a backward step. Somehow he had seemed less aggressive in the water, but now he was all male, all forceful energy, and evidently sure of himself in a way Adam could never be. But then Adam was older, more mature, and infinitely less dangerous, although how she knew this she couldn't imagine.

'Hi,' he said again, holding out his hand. 'My name's Dan Prescott. What's yours?'

Julie was taken aback. 'I don't think that's any of your business,' she exclaimed, in faintly shocked tones, making no attempt to return his gesture. 'I—er—how did you get here?'

'Motorbike,' he said laconically, bending down to push navy canvas shoes on to his feet. 'It's parked up there.' He nodded towards the trees. 'How about you?'

Julie debated whether to answer him, and then decided it would be easier if she could prove her right to be here. 'I'm staying at the hotel,' she declared distantly. 'As I told you, this land——'

'—belongs to the Kawana Point Hotel,' he finished lazily. 'Okay, so I'm trespassing. What are you going to do about it?'

Julie had no answer to that. Glancing up at him, she was intensely conscious of his size and his strength, and she didn't think she altogether trusted him. Perhaps she had been a fool to challenge him. After all, she was at least a quarter of a mile from the hotel. What could she do if he suddenly decided to attack her? No one was likely to be about at this hour of the morning.

'If—if you'll just leave, we'll say no more about it,' she said, with what she hoped sounded like calm assurance, and long thick lashes lowered to shade eyes that were the colour of the lake on a stormy day.

'And if I don't?' he countered, half amused, and Julie realised she had as much chance of controlling him as she did one of the wild cats that occasionally roamed down to the cabins in search of food.

With a helpless gesture she turned aside. His accent was confusing her again. Sometimes he sounded almost English, but at others he had a definite North America drawl. She couldn't make him out, and she was infuriatingly aware that he was getting the better of the discussion.

'You're English, aren't you?' he asked, regarding her intently. 'Are you on holiday? Or do you work at the hotel?'

'You really don't give up, do you?' she flared, giving him an angry look. 'Why don't you just go back to wherever you came from and leave me alone?'

'I'm curious.' He shrugged. 'As to where I came from —I'm staying along there . . .' He indicated the curve of the lake.

'I didn't ask,' she retorted sharply. 'I really don't care who you are or where you're staying.'

'No?' He tipped his head on one side, drops of water from his hair sliding from his jawline to the strong column of his neck. 'That's a pity, because you interest me. Besides,' the grey eyes danced, 'we're almost fellow country-men. My mother is English, too.'

'How interesting!' Julie's tone was full of sweet acid. 'Now if you'll excuse me, Mr—er——'

'Dan,' he supplied softly. 'Dan Prescott. You never did tell me your name.'

'No, I didn't.' Julie forced a faintly supercilious smile. 'Now, do you mind . . .'

'You want to swim?'

'Yes.'

'Go right ahead. Don't let me stop you.'

The inclination of his head was mocking, and Julie was infuriated. Did he really expect her to step into the water under his insolent gaze? She had no intention of giving him that advantage, and the glare she cast in his direction was venomous.

'What's the matter?' he probed. 'Afraid I may decide to join you?'

Julie tapped her foot. 'Even you wouldn't risk that. I might decide to run off with your clothes. Then what would you do?'

He grinned. 'You have a point.'

Julie sighed. 'Will you go away now?'

'Aren't you afraid I might steal your clothes?'

'I don't swim without them,' she returned sweetly.

'You should.' His lazy gaze dropped down the length of her body. 'Try it some time. There's nothing like it.'

'You're insulting!' she exclaimed.

'And you're over-reacting,' he retorted. 'Where have you been these last ten years? In a convent?'

Julie turned away, and began to scramble up the slope towards the trees. He could not know how accurate his guess had been, but it hurt all the same. Besides, it was obvious she was not going to be allowed to enjoy her swim this morning, and his particular kind of verbal fencing was alien to her.

'Wait ...'

She heard his feet crunching the shingle behind her, but she didn't turn, and when his hands suddenly caught her she panicked. No one, not even Adam, had gripped her thighs, and those hard hands encircling the flesh at the tops of her legs seemed disturbingly familiar.

'Let me go!' she cried, struggling so hard that she overbalanced both of them, his feet sliding away on the loosely packed surface, and pulling her down on top of him.

'Crazy!' he muttered, as they slid the few feet down the slope to the rocks, and Julie, trapped by the encircling pressure of his arm, was inclined to agree with him.

'If you hadn't grabbed me——!' she declared frustratedly, supremely aware of the hard muscles of his chest beneath her shoulder blades, and felt the helpless intake of breath that heralded his laughter.

'Okay, okay,' he said, as she scrambled to her feet, lying there looking up at her. 'It was a crazy thing to do. But—hell, what did I do to make you so mad at me?'

Julie pursed her lips. 'I'm not mad at you, Mr Prescott. I —I have no feelings in the matter whatsoever. I wish you'd go.'

'All right.'

With an indifferent shrug he came up beside her, and she smelt the clean male odour of his body, still damp and faintly musky. His nearness disturbed her, not least because he was barely half dressed, his shirt hanging open, his jeans low on his hips, and she could remember how he had looked in the water. He was certainly attractive, she thought, unwillingly wondering who he was. He didn't look like the guests at the hotel, who on the whole had that look of comfortable affluence, and to be riding a motorcycle in a country where everyone drove cars ... She frowned, feeling an unfamiliar tightness in her stomach, and to combat this awareness she said:

'Goodbye, then.'

He nodded, pushing the ends of his shirt into the belt of his pants, and she waited apprehensively for him to finish. But when he did, he didn't immediately move away from her. Instead he looked down at her, at the nervous twitching of her lips and lower to the unknowingly provocative rise and fall of her breasts.

'Goodbye,' he said, and before she could prevent him, he

slipped one hand around her nape and bent his mouth to hers.

Her hand came out instinctively, but encountering the taut muscles of his stomach was quickly withdrawn. She made a protesting sound deep in her throat, but he ignored it, increasing the pressure and forcing her lips apart. She felt almost giddy as her senses swam beneath his experienced caress, and then to her horror she found herself responding.

'No!'

With a cry of dismay she tore herself away from him, turning aside and scrubbing her lips with the back of her hand. She felt cheap and degraded, and appalled that just for a moment she had wanted him to go on.

'See you,' he remarked, behind her, but she didn't turn, and presently she heard his footsteps crunching up the slope to where he said he had left his motorbike.

She waited until she heard the sound of a powerful engine before venturing to look round, and then expelled her breath on a shaky sigh as she saw she was alone. He had gone, the receding roar of the motorcycle's engine indicating that he had taken the route around the lake.

Feeling slightly unsteady, Julie flopped down on to a smooth rock nearby, stretching her bare legs out to the sun. Not surprisingly, she no longer felt like going for a swim, and she wondered if she would ever come here again without remembering what had happened.

Shading her eyes, she tried to calm herself by surveying the outline of an island some distance away across the water. Everything was just the same, she told herself severely. Just because a strange man had erupted into her life and briefly disorganised it, it did not mean that she need feel any sense of guilt because of it. He had taken advantage of the situation—he was that kind of man. He was probably camping in the woods with a crowd of similarly-minded youths, all with motorcycles, and egos the size of their helmets.

With a sigh she got to her feet, picked up her towel, and scrambled back up the slope. She would swim later, she decided. Maybe she would persuade Pam's eleven-year-old son to join her. At least that way she could be reasonably sure of not being bothered.

The hotel was set on a ridge overlooking the sweep of the bay. It was a collection of log cabins, each with its own bedroom and bathroom, private suites, with meals taken in the main building close by. Backing on to the forest, with a variety of wildlife on its doorstep, it was a popular haunt for summer visitors, who moored their craft in the small marina below and climbed the stone steps to the front of the hotel. The only other approach was through the forest, but the trails were not easily defined unless one knew the way, and only occasionally did they attract visitors this way.

Pam Galloway's mother had been a friend of Mrs Osbourne, Julie's mother, and the two girls had known one another since they were children. But Pam was eight years older than Julie, and in 1967, when Julie was only ten years old, she had married a Canadian she had met on holiday in Germany, and come to live in this most beautiful part of Ontario.

Julie had missed her, but they had maintained a warm if infrequent correspondence, and when tragedy struck three months ago Pam had been first to offer her a chance to get away for a while. Canada in early summer was an enchanting place, and its distance had seemed remote from all the horrors of those weeks after her father's death. Her friends in England, her real friends, that was, had urged her to go, and with Adam's willing, if melancholy, approval, she had accepted. That had been almost a month ago now, and she knew that soon she would have to think about going back. But she didn't want to. Somehow, living here had widened her perspective, and she could no longer delude herself that everything her father had done had been for her. Returning to England would mean returning to the emptiness she had discovered her life to be, and not even Adam could make up for all those years she had lived in ignorance. She had thought her mother's death when she was twelve had unhinged him. Now she knew that only Adam's money had kept the firm together, and her father's whole existence had been a sham.

Pam and her husband, David, had their apartments in the main building. It was easier that way. It meant they were available at all hours of the day and night, and an inter-communication system connected all the cabins to the small exchange behind the desk. The reception area was already a hive of activity when Julie came in, and Pam herself hailed her from the doorway leading to the spacious dining room.

'Hi,' she exclaimed. It was the usual mode of greeting on this side of the Atlantic, and Julie was getting used to using it herself.

'Hi,' she responded, swinging her towel in her hand. 'Is that coffee I can smell brewing?'

'It sure is.' Pam wrinkled her brow as the younger girl approached her. 'You're back early. No swim?'

'No swim,' agreed Julie, not really wanting to go into details, but Pam was too inquisitive to let that go.

'Why?' she asked. 'You're not feeling sick or anything, are you? 'Cause if you are, I'll phone Doc Brewster right away.'

'No, I'm not sick.' Julie forced a smile. 'As a matter of fact, the lake was already occupied, and as I didn't feel like company ...' Her voice trailed away, and passing Pam's more generous proportions with a sideways step, she walked across the restaurant to take her usual table by the window.

The dining room was empty, but the waitresses were already about, and one of them, Penny, came to ask what she would like.

'Just toast and coffee,' Julie assured her firmly, aware of Pam's enquiring face in the background, and the girl knew better than to offer the steak or eggs or maple syrup pancakes that so many of their visitors seemed to enjoy.

'Well?' Pam prompted, coming to stand with plump arms folded, looking down at her young friend. She had put on weight since her marriage to David, and having sampled the meals served at the Kawana Point Hotel, Julie wasn't really surprised. Steaks tended to weigh at least half a pound, with matching helpings of baked potatoes or french fries to go with them, while the desserts of cream-filled pastries or mouthwatering American cheesecake simply added inches just looking at them. Julie felt sure she, too, would burst at the seams if she enjoyed their hospitality for much longer, although her own level of metabolism seemed to dispute this anxiety.

'Well, what?' she said now, hoping Pam was not going to be difficult, but the other girl seemed determined to discover the facts.

'Who was occupying the lake? No one from the hotel, I'm sure. I didn't know anyone else knew of that cove.'

'Nor did I,' replied Julie, playing with the cutlery. 'But obviously we were wrong.'

'So who was it?' Pam persisted. 'Not campers? There's barely room to pitch a tent.'

'No, not campers,' Julie assured her resignedly. 'It was just some man, a tourist, I suppose. He said he was staying down the far end of the bend in the lake near the cove.'

'You spoke to him?' Pam was interested, taking the seat opposite her and gazing at her with twinkling eyes. 'Hey, how about that? All these weeks you've rebuffed every introduction we've arranged for you, and now you go and meet some guy down at the lake!'

'It wasn't like that,' declared Julie wearily, wishing she had played invalid after all. 'He was just—swimming, and —well, he spoke to me. It was all perfectly innocent and certainly nothing for you to get so excited about.'

Or was it? Julie couldn't prevent the unwilling surge of some emotion along her veins, and the remembrance of how he had held her and kissed her brought goose-bumps out all over her body. Hoping Pam would attribute them to the chilly air-conditioning of the dining room and not to any other cause, she folded her arms on the table and surreptitiously looped her fingers over the most obvious flesh on her upper arms.

'So who is he?' Pam urged her, arching her blonde brows. 'Did he give you his name?' She frowned. 'I don't know who he might be staying with. The Leytons and the Peruccis have summer places along there, but they don't normally associate with the common crowd.'

'Pam, it was no one like that.' Julie shook her head. 'He was riding a motorcycle, or'—she added blushing—'he said he was. He just wasn't the type you think.'

'Ah, older, you mean?'

'No. Younger.' Julie looked up in relief as Penny brought her toast and coffee. 'Mmmm, this is just what I needed. It's quite chilly in here, isn't it?'

Pam waited until Penny had departed and then looked at her impatiently. 'So what was his name? Did you get it?'

Julie sighed. 'Prescott,' she said reluctantly. 'Dan Prescott.'

'No!'

Pam was regarding her in disbelief now, and Julie wished she would go away and stop making a fuss about nothing. It was bad enough having her morning disrupted, without Pam sitting there looking as if she had just delivered her a body blow.

'Pam, look, I know you mean well, but I am going to marry Adam, you know. It's all arranged. Just as soon as I feel able——'

'Julie, did he really say his name was Dan Prescott?' Pam interrupted her, leaning across the table, her hand on the younger girl's wrist preventing her from putting the wedge of toast she had just buttered into her mouth.

Julie pulled her hand free and nodded. 'That's what he said.'

Pam shook her head. 'My God!'

Julie regarded her half irritably now. 'What's wrong with that?' she demanded, popping the wedge of toast into her mouth, and wiping her fingers on her napkin. 'It's a common enough name, isn't it? I mean, he's not an escaped convict or anything, is he?' Her features sobered somewhat at the thought.

'No, no.' Pam shook her head vigorously now, half getting up from her chair and then flopping down again as she realised Julie deserved some explanation. 'Julie, Dan Prescott is Anthea Leyton's nephew!' She made an excited little movement of her hands. 'Anthea Leyton was a Prescott before she got married, and the New York Prescotts *are* the Scott National Bank!'

Julie put down her knife and lay back in her seat. 'So what?'

'So *what?*' Pam licked her lips. 'Julie, don't you realise, you've been talking to Lionel Prescott's son!'

In spite of herself, Julie's nerves prickled at the thought. The names meant nothing to her, but banking did, and judging by Pam's awed expression the Prescotts were no ordinary banking house. New York bankers tended to be immensely rich, and she had no doubt that it was this which had stunned her friend.

Forcing herself to act naturally, she poured another cup of coffee, and taking the cup between her cold fingers she said: 'I rather fancy you might be wrong, Pam. He—er—he said his mother was English, not American.'

'No, she's not!' Pam was really excited now. 'Heavens, that confirms it, doesn't it? Sheila Prescott is English. I think she was only a debutante when they met. You know how these stories get around.'

Julie took a deep breath. 'Well——' She tried to appear nonchalant. 'I've provided a little bit of gossip to brighten up your day.'

'Julie!' Pam looked at her reprovingly. 'Don't say you're not impressed, because I won't believe it. I mean—imagine meeting Dan Prescott! What was he doing here? What did he say?'

Julie put down her cup as David Galloway came into the dining room looking for his wife. He grinned when he saw them sitting together by the window, but before he could say anything Pam launched into an extravagant description of how Julie had made friends with Anthea Leyton's nephew.

'That's not true,' Julie felt bound to contradict her, looking apologetically at David. 'As a matter of fact, I was rather rude to him. I—er—I told him this was private land.'

'Good for you!' David was not half as awed as his wife, and she adopted an aggrieved air.

'You know how Margie Laurence always talks about the Leytons going into her store,' she protested, getting up from the table. 'Well, I'm looking forward to seeing her face when I tell her about Julie.'

'Oh, no, Pam, you can't!' Julie was horrified, imagining Dan Prescott's reaction if the story ever got to his ears. Pam had no idea what she was dealing with, but she did, and her face burned at the thought of being gossiped about in the local chandlery. 'Please—forget I ever told you!'

'You've got to do it, Pam,' David asserted, shaking his head. 'Besides, if what Julie says is true, the least said about this the better.' He grimaced. 'Just remember, we lease this land from the Leytons, and I'd hate to do anything that might offend them.'

Pam looked sulky. 'You mean I can't tell anyone?'

'What's to tell?' exclaimed Julie helplessly. 'Pam, I'm sorry, but I wish I'd never told you.'

Pam hunched her shoulders. 'But Dan Prescott, Julie!

Imagine it! Imagine *dating* Dan Prescott!'

Julie gazed at her incredulously. 'There was never any question of that, Pam. Besides, have you forgotten Adam?'

'Adam? Oh, Adam!' Pam dismissed him with an impatient gesture. 'Adam's too old for you, Julie, and if you were honest with yourself, you'd admit it.'

'*Pam!*'

David was horrified at his wife's lack of discretion, and even Julie was a little embarrassed at the bluntness of her tone. It seemed that meeting with Dan Prescott had been fated from the start, and now she was left in the awkward position of having to accept the apologies David was insisting Pam should make.

'All right,' she was saying, when he nudged her to continue, 'I know it's not my business, but—well, I'm only thinking of you, Julie. Adam was your *father's* partner, after all, and he's at least old enough to take over that role. Are you sure that's not what you were thinking of when you accepted his proposal?'

There was another pregnant pause, and then, to Julie's relief, the Edens came into the restaurant, the children's voices disrupting the silence with strident shrillness. It meant Pam had a reason to go and summon the waitresses, and David, left with Julie, squeezed her shoulder sympathetically.

'She means well,' he muttered gruffly, his open face revealing his confusion, but Julie only smiled.

'I know,' she said, grimacing as one of the Eden boys started doing a Red Indian war-dance around the tables. 'Don't worry, David. I've known Pam too long to take offence, and besides, I have disappointed her.'

'Over the Prescott boy? Yes, I know.' David shook his head. 'Take my word, you're well out of it, Julie. I wouldn't like to think any daughter of mine was mixed up with him. I don't know how true it is, but I hear he's been quite a hell-raiser since he left college, and there's been more scandal attached to the Prescott name . . .'

'You don't have to tell me all this, David,' Julie said gently. 'I'm not interested in Dan Prescott, and he's not interested in me. We—we met, by accident—and that's all.'

'I'm glad.'

David patted her shoulder and then excused himself to attend to his other guests, leaving Julie to finish her breakfast in peace. But as with the swim earlier, her appetite had left her, and despite her assertion to the contrary, she could not help pondering why a man with all the lake to choose from should have swum in her special place, and at her special time.

CHAPTER TWO

JULIE'S cabin was just the same as all the other cabins, except that in the month she had been there she had added a few touches of her own. There was the string of Indian beads she had draped over the lampshade, so that when the lamp was on, the light picked out the vivid colours of the vegetable dye; the Eskimo doll who sat on the table by her bed, snug and warm in his sealskin coat and fur cap; and the motley assortment of paperweights and key-rings and ashtrays—chunky glass baubles, with scenes of Ontario imprisoned within their transparent exteriors.

The cabins were simply but comfortably furnished. The well-sprung divans had natural wood headboards, and the rest of the bedroom furniture was utilitarian. There was a closet, a chest of drawers with a mirror above, a table and chairs, and one easy chair. The bathroom was fitted with a shower unit above the bath, and there was always plenty of hot water. Julie had discovered that Canadians expected this facility and remembering the lukewarm baths she had taken in English hotels, she thought they could well learn something from them. Everything was spotlessly clean, both in the cabins and in the main building, and the staff were always ready and willing to accommodate her every need. She would miss their cheerful friendliness when she returned to England, she thought, still unable to contemplate that eventuality without emotion.

Changing for dinner that evening, Julie viewed the becoming tan she was acquiring with some pleasure. She had looked so pale and drained of all colour when she had arrived, but now her cheeks were filling out a little with all the rich food Pam was pressing on her, and she no longer had that waif-like appearance.

Regarding her reflection as she applied a dark mascara to her lashes, she decided Adam would see a definite change in her. She had grown accustomed to seeing a magnolia-pale face in the mirror, with sharply-defined features and honey-coloured hair. Now she had a different image, the thin features rounded out, the hair bleached by the sun and streaked with gold. She had not had it cut for months, and instead of her usual ear-length bob it had lengthened and thickened, and it presently swung about her shoulders, curling back from her face in a style that was distinctly becoming.

She had not troubled much about clothes either since she left England. Most of the time she wore shorts or jeans, adding an embroidered smock or tunic at night instead of the cotton vests she wore during the day. Adam, who had always complimented her on her dress sense at home, would be appalled if he could see her now, she thought ruefully, putting down the mascara brush and studying herself critically. He did not approve of the negligent morals of the younger generation, and in his opinion the casual attitude towards appearance was equally contemptible. Still, Julie consoled herself wryly, she had paid little heed to what she had thrown into her suitcases before she left London, and because what she had brought was unsuitable to her surroundings, she had bought the cheapest and most serviceable substitutes available.

Now she turned away from the mirror, and checked that she had her keys. They were in the pocket of her jeans, and she adjusted the cords that looped the bottom of her cheesecloth shirt before leaving the cabin.

It was a mild night, the air delightfully soft and redolent with the scents of the forest close by. She crossed the square to the main building with deliberate slowness, anticipating what she would have for dinner with real enthusiasm, and climbed the shallow stairs to the swing doors with growing confidence. These weeks had done wonders for her, she acknowledged, and she felt an immense debt of gratitude towards Pam and her husband.

The reception hall was brightly illuminated, even though it was not yet dark outside. Already there were sounds of activity from the dining room, and the small bar adjoining was doing a good trade. Julie acknowledged the greeting of the young receptionist, a biology student working his vacation, and then was almost laid flat by an energetic young body bursting out of the door that led to the Galloways' private apartments. It was Brad Galloway, Pam's twelve-year-old son, and already he was almost as broad as his father.

'Hey ...'

Julie protested, and Brad pulled an apologetic face. 'I'm sorry,' he gasped. 'But there's a terrific yacht coming into the marina! D'you want to come and see?'

'I don't think so, thank you.' Julie's refusal was dry. 'And you won't make it if you go headlong down the steps.'

'I won't.' Brad exhibited the self-assurance that all Canadian children seemed to have and charged away towards the doors. 'See you, Julie!' he called and was gone, leaving Julie to exchange a rueful grimace with the young man behind the desk.

'I know—*kids*!' he grinned, not averse to flirting with an attractive girl, so far without any success. 'Did he hurt you? Can I do anything for you?'

'I don't think so, thank you.' Julie's lips twitched. 'I think a long cool drink is in order, and Pietro can supply me with that.'

Pietro, the bartender, was an Italian who had emigrated to Canada more than twenty years ago, yet he still retained his distinctive accent. He had been quite a Lothario in his time, but at fifty-three his talents were limited, and Julie enjoyed his amusing chatter. His wife, Rosa, worked in the kitchens, and their various offspring were often to be seen about the hotel.

'So, little Julie,' he said, as she squeezed on to a stool at the bar. 'What have you been doing with yourself today?'

Julie smiled. 'What do I usually do?' she countered, hedging her shoulder against the press of George Fairley's broad back. He and his wife were always in the bar at this hour, and invariably hogged the counter. 'Yes, the same as ever,' she nodded, as Pietro held up a bottle of Coke. 'With plenty of ice, please.'

'Wouldn't you like me to put you something a little sharper in here?' Pietro suggested, pulling a very expressive face. 'A little rum perhaps, or——'

'No, thanks.' Julie shook her head, her smile a little tight now. 'I—er—I'm not fond of alcohol. I don't like what it can do to people.' She gave a faint apologetic smile, circling the glass he pushed towards her with her fingers. 'It's been another lovely day, hasn't it?'

Pietro shrugged, a typically continental gesture, and accepted her change of topic without comment. 'A lovely day,' he echoed. 'A lovely day for a lovely girl,' he added teasingly. 'You know, Julie, if I were ten years younger ...'

'And not married,' she murmured obediently, and he laughed. They had played this game before. But, as always, she saw the gleam of speculation in his eyes, and picking up her glass she made her exit, carrying it with her into the dining room.

She chose a shrimp cocktail to start with. These shellfish were enormous, huge juicy morsels served with a barbecue sauce that added a piquant flavour all its own. When Julie first came to Kawana Point, she had found herself satisfied after only one course, but now she could order a sirloin steak and salad without feeling unduly greedy.

She was dipping a luscious shrimp into the barbecue sauce when she looked up and saw two men crossing the reception hall towards the bar. Her table was situated by

the window, but it was in line with double doors that
opened into the hall, and she had an unobstructed view of
anyone coming or going. The fact that she averted her eyes
immediately did not prevent her identification of one of the
men, and her hand trembled uncontrollably, causing the
shrimp to drop completely into the strongly-flavoured
sauce.

Putting down her fork, she wiped her lips with her napkin, trying desperately to retain her self-composure. What
was Dan Prescott doing here? she wondered anxiously.
People like the Prescotts did not visit hotels like the Kawana
Point. They stayed at their own summer residences, and
when they needed entertainment they went into Orillia or
Barrie, or to any one of a dozen private clubs situated along
the lake shore road.

Her taste for the shrimps dwindling, she picked up her
glass and swallowed a mouthful of Coke. It was coolly re-
freshing, and as she put down her glass again she felt a
growing impatience with herself. What was she? Some kind
of cipher or something? Just because a man she had never
expected to see again had turned up at the hotel it did not
mean he had come in search of her. That was the most ap-
palling conceit, and totally unlike her. Was it unreasonable
that having discovered the whereabouts of the hotel he
should come and take a look at it, but how had he got here
this time? She had not heard any motorcycle, a sound
which would carry on the evening air, and although he was
not wearing evening clothes he had been wearing an
expensive-looking jacket, hardly the attire for two wheels.

Appalled anew that she should remember so distinctly
what he had been wearing after such a fleeting appraisal,
Julie determinedly picked up her fork again. Then she remembered the yacht, the yacht which had aroused such excitement from the normally-laconic Brad. Was that how
they had made the trip across to the hotel?

The appearance of Pam in her working gear of cotton

shirt and denims, her plump face flushed and excited, did nothing to improve her digestion. Her friend came bustling towards her, and it was obvious from her manner that she knew exactly who was in the bar.

'Did you see him?' she hissed, bending over Julie's table, and the younger girl deliberately bit the tail from a shrimp before replying.

'See who?' she asked then, playing for time, but Pam was not deceived.

'You must have seen them cross the hall,' she whispered impatiently, casting an apologetic glance at her other residents. 'They're in the bar. What are you going to do?'

Julie looked bland. 'What am *I* going to do?' she echoed.

'Yes.' Pam sighed. 'Well, I mean it's obvious, isn't it? He didn't come here just to taste the beer. His cousin's with him—at least, I think it's his cousin. He calls him Drew, and I know Anthea Leyton has a son called Andrew——'

'Pam, their being here has nothing to do with me,' declared Julie firmly. 'If they choose to come—to come slumming, that's their affair. I have no intention of speaking to Dan Prescott, so don't go getting any ideas.'

'But, Julie, you can't just ignore him!'

'Why not?' Julie hid her trembling hands beneath the napkin in her lap. 'Honestly, Pam, I don't even like the man!'

'You said yourself, you hardly know him.'

'All the more reason for keeping out of his way.'

'Well, I think you're crazy!'

'Oh, do you?' Julie stared up at her, half irritated by her insistence.

'Yes.' Pam dismissed the younger girl's objections with an inconsequent wave of her hand. 'Julie, you may never get another chance to meet him socially——'

'I don't want that chance, Pam.'

'Why?'

'Because I'm not interested.'

Pam gazed at her disbelievingly. 'You mean you're afraid.'

'Afraid?' Julie gasped.

'Yes, afraid.' Pam straightened, resting her hands on her broad hips. 'You've had your life organised for you for so long, you've forgotten what it's like to take a risk——'

'So you admit it is a risk?'

Julie tilted her head, and Pam pulled a wry face. 'All right. So he does have a reputation. What of it? You're an adult, aren't you. You can handle it.'

Julie sighed. 'I don't want to handle anything, Pam. I just want to sit here and eat my dinner, and afterwards I'm going to watch some television and then go to bed.'

Pam made a defeated gesture. 'I give up.'

'Good.'

Julie determinedly returned to her shrimp cocktail and Pam had no alternative but to leave her to it. But she shook her head rather frustratedly as she crossed to the door, and Julie, watching her, doubted she had heard the last of it.

By the time she had eaten half a dozen mouthfuls of her steak, she knew she was fighting a losing battle. The awareness of the man in the bar, of the possibility that he might choose to come into the dining room and order a meal, filled her with unease, and she knew she would not feel secure until she was safely locked behind her cabin door.

Declining a dessert, she left her table, walking swiftly through the open doors into the reception area. It was usually deserted at this hour of the evening, most of the guests either occupying the dining room or the bar, and she expected to make her escape unobserved. What she had not anticipated was Brad Galloway, deep in conversation with the man she most wanted to avoid, or to be involved in that discussion by the boy's artless invitation.

'Julie!' he exclaimed, when he saw her. 'Do you remember that yacht I told you about? Well, this is Mr Prescott who owns it.'

'I didn't say that, Brad.' Dan Prescott's voice was just as disturbing as she remembered. 'I said it belonged to my family. It does. I just have the use of it now and then.'

His grin was apologetic, both to the boy and to Julie, but she refused to respond to it. In fact, she refused to look at Dan Prescott at all after that first dismaying appraisal. Yet, for all that, she knew the exact colour of the bluish-grey corded jacket he was wearing, and the way the dark blue jeans hugged the contours of his thighs. His clothes were casual, but they fitted him well, and she realised something she had not realised before. Men like Dan Prescott did not need to exhibit their wealth. They accepted it. It was a fact. And that extreme self-confidence was all the proof they needed.

'What do you say, Julie?'

Brad was looking at her a little querulously now, and she forced herself to show the enthusiasm he was expecting. 'That's great,' she murmured, realising her words sounded artificial even to her ears. 'You must tell me all about it tomorrow.'

'Why not right now?'

The words could have been Brad's, but they weren't, and Julie was obliged to acknowledge Dan Prescott's presence for the first time. Even so, it was almost a physical shock meeting that penetrating stare. The lapse of time had been too brief for her to forget a second of their last encounter, and it was only too easy to remember how she had had to tear herself away from him, breaking the intimate contact he had initiated. Nevertheless, she had broken the contact, she told herself firmly, and he had no right to do this to her. But as his eyes moved lower, over the firm outline of her breasts and the rounded swell of her hips, she felt a wave of heat flooding over her, and nothing could alter the fact that if she were as indifferent to him as she liked to think, it wouldn't matter what he did.

With a feeling of mortification she felt his eyes come back

to her face, and then the heavy lids drooped. 'Why not right now?' he repeated, as aware of her confusion as she was herself, and conscious of Brad's puzzled stare Julie tried to pull herself together.

'I—why, I don't have time just now, Brad,' she offered, addressing her apology to the boy. 'Some other time perhaps . . .'

'Okay.'

Brad shrugged, obviously disappointed, and she was sorry, but then, to add to her humiliation, Pam appeared. It only took her a couple of seconds to sum up the situation, and acting purely on instinct Julie was sure, she exclaimed:

'Oh, there you are, Brad. I've been looking for you.' Her smile flashed briefly at Dan Prescott. 'Come along, I want you to help me hang those lamps in the yard.'

'Oh, *Mom*!'

Brad's voice was eloquent with feeling, and after only a slight hesitation Dan said: 'Perhaps I could help you, Mrs Galloway.'

Pam was obviously taken aback, but Julie's hopes of reprieve were quickly squashed. 'That won't be necessary, Mr Prescott, thank you,' her friend assured him warmly. 'Brad will do it—he always does. He's such a help around the place.'

'I'm sure he is.' Dan's expression was amused as it rested on the boy's mutinous face. 'Sorry, old son, but there'll be another time.'

'Will there? Will there really?'

Brad gazed up at him eagerly, and with a fleeting glance in Julie's direction Dan nodded. 'You have my word on it,' he nodded, pushing his hands into his jacket pockets, and Brad's demeanour was swiftly transformed.

'Oh—*boy*!' he exclaimed, and grinned almost defiantly at Julie before his mother ushered him away.

But when Julie would have left too, lean brown fingers looped themselves loosely around her wrist. 'Wait . . .'

The word was uttered somewhere near her temple, and the warmth of his breath ruffled the strands of silky hair that lay across her forehead. It was a husky injunction, a soft invocation to delay her while Pam and her son got out of earshot, yet when she tried to release herself his fingers reacted like a slip knot that tightened the more it was strained against. His command might have been mild, but it was a command nevertheless, she realised, and she was forced to stand there, supremely aware that if she moved her fingers they would brush his leg.

'So,' he said at last, when they were alone, the student receptionist having departed to take his dinner some time before, 'why are you running out on me?'

Julie contemplated denying the allegation, but she had no desire to start an argument with him. Besides, he was experienced enough to know if she was lying, and opposition often provoked an interest that otherwise would not have been there.

'Why do you think?' she asked instead, assuming a bored expression, and the long thick lashes came to shade his eyes.

'You tell me,' he suggested, and with a sigh she said: 'Because I don't want to get involved with you, Mr Prescott.'

'I see.' His look was quizzical.

'Now will you let me go?'

He frowned. 'Why don't you like me? What did I do to provoke such a reaction?'

'I neither like nor dislike you, Mr Prescott,' she retorted twisting her wrist impotently. 'Please let go of me.'

'Is all this outraged modesty because I kissed you?'

'I'd rather not discuss it.' Julie held up her head. 'I don't know why you're here, Mr Prescott, but I'd prefer it if you'd forget we ever met before.'

'Would you?' The smoky grey eyes drooped briefly to her

mouth, and it was an almost tangible incursion. 'Would you really?'

'Yes,' but Julie had to grind her teeth together to say it. When he looked at her like that she found it incredibly difficult to keep a clear head, and almost desperately she sought for a means of diversion. 'I—where is your cousin? Won't he be wondering where you are?'

'Drew?' Dan Prescott's look changed to one of mocking inquiry. 'How did you know I came with Drew?' His eyes narrowed. 'Do you know him?'

'Of course not.' Too late Julie realised she had made a mistake. 'I—er—I saw the two of you come in, that's all. And—and Pam said something about him being your cousin.'

'Pam? Oh—Mrs Galloway, of course.' With a shrug he released her, but as she moved to go past him he stepped into her path. 'One more thing . . .'

'What?'

'I want you to come out with me tomorrow.'

The invitation was not entirely unexpected, but its delivery was, and Julie felt a sense of stunned indignation that he should think it would be that easy.

'No,' she said, without hesitation.

'Why not?'

He was persistent, and she found it was impossible to get by him without his co-operation. 'Because—because I don't want to,' she retorted shortly. 'I've told you——'

'—you don't want to get involved with me, I know.' He pulled his upper lip between his teeth. 'But you don't really believe that any more than I do.'

'Mr Prescott——'

'And stop calling me *Mr* Prescott. You know my name, just as I now know yours—Julie.'

Julie found she was trembling. This verbal fencing was more exhausting than she had thought, and she looked round helplessly, wishing for once that Pam would interfere. But apart from the Meades, who were leaving the dining room with their arms wrapped around each other, there was no one to appeal to, and she could not intrude on their evident self-absorption.

'Why are you fighting me?' Dan's breath fanned her ear as she turned back to look at him, and an involuntary shiver swept over her. 'Come and have a drink,' he invited. 'I'll introduce you to my cousin, and then perhaps you might begin to believe my father wasn't the devil incarnate!'

'You—you're——'

'Disgusting? Yes, you told me. But I can be fun too, if you'll let me.'

The grey eyes had darkened and Julie felt her heart slow and then quicken to a suffocating pace. Oh God, she thought weakly, he knows exactly how to get what he wants, and she didn't know whether she had the strength to resist him.

'I—I can't,' she got out through her dry throat. 'I can't.'

'Okay.'

With a laconic shrug it was over. Almost before she was aware of it, he had moved past her, walking with lithe indolence towards the bar where his cousin was waiting, and she was free to go.

With her breath coming in tortured gasps, she practically ran across the hall, dropping down the two shallow steps that led to the swing doors, going through them with such force that they continued to swing long after she had left them. She didn't stop until she was inside her cabin, but even then she did not feel the sense of security she had expected.

CHAPTER THREE

JULIE did not go down to the lake to swim again for almost a week. It was foolish because she had no reason to suppose that Dan Prescott might be there, but a necessary interval seemed called for, and she contented herself with going out with Brad in his dinghy, or taking the controls of his father's power boat so that he could water-ski. He was quite good at it, but although Julie tried, she persistently lost her balance and ended up choking for breath in the power-boat's wake.

Eventually, however, common-sense overrode her nervousness, and she returned to her early morning pastime. Dan Prescott had not come back to the hotel, and although she had succeeded in evading Pam's more personal questions about what had happened between them that night, her continued abstinence was provoking comment. So she began to make her regular morning trek to the cove, and after three days of solitude she began to believe she would never see him again.

Then, on the fourth morning, he appeared.

Julie was already in the water, swimming vigorously across the mouth of the inlet, when she saw the tall figure standing motionless on the rocks. As before, he was dressed in denim jeans and shirt, and even as she watched, he peeled off his shirt and tossed it on to the rocks. She turned quickly away before he unbuckled the belt of his pants. She had no desire to see him naked, and the awareness that he was coming into the water with her filled her with trembling anticipation.

There was no way she could get out without passing him. Around the mouth of the inlet there were currents she wasn't familiar with, and besides, it was a good half mile round and into the next cove where David had built his marina. She was trapped, and he knew it. No doubt he had planned it this way deliberately. And she despised him for it.

She heard the splash as he entered the water and permitted herself a backward glance. He was nowhere in sight, probably swimming underwater, she thought apprehensively, and then almost lost her breath when he surfaced right beside her.

'Hi!'

Julie drew a trembling breath. 'Don't you ever give up?'

'It's a free country, isn't it?' His eyes mocked her. 'Or are you going to tell me the land is private?'

'I know your uncle owns it, if that's what you mean,' Julie retorted, pushing back her hair with an unsteady hand. 'Enjoy your swim. You'll be happy to know you've spoilt mine!'

The word he said was not polite, and his hands reached for her before she could defend herself, pulling her down into the water until her nasal tubes were blocked and she thought her lungs were going to burst. Then he let her go, allowing her to float up to the surface, gulping desperately for breath as he came up behind her.

'That—that was a rotten thing to do,' she got out, when she could speak again, and he made no attempt to deny it. 'I could have drowned!'

He seemed to consider her protest for a few seconds and then he shook his head. 'I don't think I could have allowed that,' he remarked, in all seriousness. 'Great though the temptation might be.'

Julie pursed her lips. 'You enjoy making fun of me, don't you?'

'I enjoy—you,' he said, slowly and deliberately so that her whole body seemed suffused with heat, in spite of the coldness of the water. 'Or rather I would—if you'd let me.'

There was a brief pause while Julie's green eyes stared in troubled fascination into his, and then with panic quickening her limbs she struck out blindly for the shore. It was useless, she told herself, she could not have an ordinary conversation with him. He persisted in turning every innocent remark into something personal, and her inexperience in these matters made her an easy target. She should have known he would not let her be. He was a predator, and right now she was his prey. And like all hunters, the harder the chase, the more satisfying the kill.

Her feet found the stony lake shore, and she waded up out of the water on slightly wobbly legs. The exertion had been all the more tiring because of her awareness of him behind her, and the fear that at any moment he might grab her flailing feet. However, she made it unscathed, though as she groped for her towel she heard him emerge from the water behind her.

Squeezing the excess moisture from her hair, she tried to ignore him, but he walked across the shingle and sprawled lazily on a flat rock. Almost compulsively, her eyes were drawn to him, and his lips curved in amusement at that involuntary appraisal. It was obvious from the apprehensiveness of her darting glance that she had expected the worst, but to her relief she saw he was wearing thin navy shorts, and although they left little to her imagination, he was decently covered.

'You didn't really think I'd do that, did you?' he enquired, propping himself up on one elbow and regarding her bikini-clad figure quizzically.

'Do what?' Julie was evasive, towelling her hair with more effort than skill, wondering if she could wriggle into her shorts without making a spectacle of herself.

'Swim in the raw,' Dan answered bluntly, knowing full well she was not unaware of his meaning. 'I wouldn't want to embarrass you a second time.'

'You didn't embarrass me, Mr Prescott,' Julie retorted,

not altogether truthfully, deciding the shorts would have
to wait until she had gained the privacy of the trees.
'Goodbye!'

'Julie ...' With a lithe movement, he sprang off the
rocks and caught her arm as she bent to pick up her be-
longings. 'Julie, don't go. Look, I'm sorry if I've offended
you, but for heaven's sake, what's a guy got to do to make
it with you?'

Julie gathered her towel and shorts to her chest almost
as if they were a shield, and avoided looking up at him.
'Mr Prescott, I don't know the kind of girls you are used
to associating with, but men don't—*make it* with me, as
you so crudely put it. Just because you're apparently
accustomed to every girl you meet falling flat on her face
when you show an interest in them, don't——'

'Why not flat on their backs?' he interrupted her harshly.
'That would facilitate matters, wouldn't it?' and her breathing quickened to a suffocating pace.

'As I said, you're——'

'Forget it!' he snapped. 'I don't know why I came here.'

'Because you can't bear to think you're not irresistible!'
Julie retorted recklessly, and then quivered uncontrollably
as he tore the towel and shorts from her fingers and jerked
her towards him.

His hands gripping the flesh of her upper arms were hard
and painful, imprisoning her within their savage embrace
and numbing her resistance. When he bent his head towards her, she had no hope of avoiding him and although
she turned her head from side to side, he found her mouth
with unerring accuracy, fastening his lips to hers and taking
his fill of her honeyed softness. His damp body was an
aggressive barrier to any escape she might attempt to make,
and try as she might, she could not prevent the awareness
of her breasts hardening against the forceful expanse of his
chest.

It was impossible, too, to prevent him from parting her

lips. Choking for breath, she gulped for air against his mouth, but the invasion of his lips robbed her of all opposition. He was devouring her, hungrily teaching her the meaning of the adult emotions he was arousing, and as her lips began to kiss him back, the pressure eased to a paralysing sweetness. His hands released her arms to slide across her back, and her legs trembled as he pressed her body into his. She could feel him with every nerve and sinew of her being, and the growing awareness of what was happening to him made her acutely aware of the fragile barrier between herself and his thrusting masculinity.

He released her mouth to seek the hollow behind her ear, kissing her earlobe and her neck, brushing her hair aside to stroke the sensitive curve of her nape with his tongue. Julie knew she ought to draw back, that this was her opportunity to get away from him, but she was consumed by the urgency of her own emotions, and too aroused to think sensibly about anything.

The bra of her bikini slackened as he released the clip, and a silent protest rose inside her as his fingers found the rose-tipped mounds that no man had ever seen before, let alone touched.

'Don't ...' he said, as her hands sought to obstruct him. 'Don't stop me. Oh, Julie, you're beautiful!'

'Am I?'

Her breath came in little gasps and his mouth curved in sensuous approval. 'You know it,' he groaned, his lips against her creamy flesh. 'Oh, God, what am I going to do about you?'

'Do about me?' she echoed confusedly, but his mouth covered hers once again, silencing any further speculation. The urgency of his caress drove all coherent thought from her head, and soft arms wound around his neck in eager submission.

Her convent upbringing had not prepared her for this, or for the unexpected sensuality of her own nature, and her instinctive response was all the more unrestrained because of it. She was warm and soft and responsive, her silky body yielding to his with innocent fervour, and Dan almost lost his own grip on sanity as he continued to hold her. She was so completely desirable, so eminently responsive to his every overture, and the urge to lower her to the rocks and submerge himself in her honeyed softness was almost overpowering. He doubted she would oppose him. She was all melting passion in his arms. But if he had been overwhelmed by her artless submission, he was still rational enough to realise that she was not entirely aware of what she was inviting. He could imagine her reaction when she came to her senses, and she would resent him bitterly if he took advantage of her innocence.

For all that, it was incredibly difficult to resist her, and a groan was forced from him as he compelled her away. Then, avoiding her look of hurt bewilderment, he bent and picked up her towel, pressing it into her fingers with a rough insensitivity.

Julie was mortified, as much by the awareness of her own wanton behaviour as by the realisation that he had given her the towel to cover her nakedness. He had taken advantage of her, and she had encouraged him, and what was more humiliating, he had rejected her.

'I'm sorry.' His apology came strangely to her ears, and her averted gaze turned blindly from the shocked realisation that he was no less aroused than before. 'But—well, I guess I lost my head,' he muttered half reluctantly, 'and I guess you did too.'

Julie licked her dry lips. 'Lost your head?' she echoed, as his meaning became clear to her. 'But I wouldn't——'

'Yes, you would,' he retorted harshly. 'We're not children, Julie, and you know I want you. However, aside from other considerations, I don't honestly know what you want.'

Julie blinked, trying to make sense of what he was saying to her. It appeared she was wrong. He had not rejected her because of any inadequacy on her part. He had actually considered the possibility, but because he was more experienced, he had dismissed the idea. There was something horribly cold-blooded about the whole affair, and her head moved helplessly from side to side as she bent to retrieve her discarded bra.

'Julie!' He was speaking to her again, but she refused to answer him. She just wanted to get away, the farther away the better, and she struggled wildly when he endeavoured to detain her. '*Julie!*' he said again, more forcefully this time. 'Julie, listen to me! When am I going to see you again? Today? Tonight? When?'

'Never, I hope,' she choked, throwing back her head, her hair cascading damply about her shoulders. 'Just let me go——'

'No, I won't.' He thrust his impatient face close to hers. 'You're not being sensible, Julie, and I don't intend to let you go until you are!'

'I'll scream——'

'In that state?' His mocking eyes flicked the slipping ends of the towel and her face suffused with colour. But all the humour had left his expression, and he was deadly serious as he said: 'Okay, you want the truth, you got it. When I'm with you, I can't think sanely.' His eyes burned above her. 'But unlike you, I accept that people have feelings, and I didn't want to hurt you.'

Julie faltered. 'To—hurt me?'

'Yes, damn you,' he muttered, unable to prevent himself from pulling her to him again. 'There,' he added hoarsely, 'now tell me you don't know what I'm feeling—you're not that naïve. But I do know you've never been with a man before, even if you do learn fast.'

Julie's tongue appeared in unknowing provocation. 'I—I don't understand ...'

'Don't you?' His hands slipped possessively around her waist, hard and warm against the cooler skin of her hips.

'Could you have stopped me? Honestly?' He bent his head to her shoulder, his teeth gently massaging the soft flesh. 'But wouldn't you have hated me if I had?'

Julie's face burned. 'You shouldn't say such things!'

'Why not?' Dan lifted his head to gaze intently down at her. 'It's a fact.'

Julie drew an uneven breath. 'Let me go, Dan.'

Her husky request brought a faint smile to his lips. 'At last,' he murmured. 'I wondered what I'd have to do to get you to say my name.'

'Dan, please ...'

Julie pressed her hands determinedly against his chest, but the hair-roughened skin was absurdly sensuous against her palms, and she stood there helpless in the grip of emotions she scarcely knew or understood.

'Tonight,' he said, his breath fanning her cheek as he bent towards her. 'Have dinner with me, on the yacht. We can serve ourselves—just the two of us.'

'I can't.'

The denial sprang automatically to her lips, and his mouth turned down at the corners. 'Why not?'

'Because I can't.' Julie freed herself from him without too much difficulty, and quickly slipped her arms into the bra, fastening the clip with trembling fingers. Then, gathering up her shorts and the towel, she turned back to him. 'G-goodbye.'

If she had expected him to object as he had done before, she was disappointed. With a weary shrug of his shoulders he bent to pick up his own pants, and thrust his legs into them without giving her another glance. It was as if he had grown bored with the whole exchange, and as on that evening at the hotel, he had abandoned the struggle.

Conversely, Julie was left feeling strangely bereft, and stepping into her sandals she made her way across the shingle with a distinct sense of deprivation.

The feeling had not left her by the time she reached

the hotel, but in the sanctuary of her cabin she faced the fact that she had probably had the most lucky escape ever. As her blood cooled, reaction set in, and she sank down on to the bed trembling at the realisation of how near she had come to losing all respect for herself and betraying Adam's trust in her. She didn't know what had come over her, and for someone who for so long had regarded herself as immune from the kind of behaviour gossiped about in the dormitory after lights-out, it was doubly humiliating. She would never have thought she might have reason to be grateful to Dan Prescott, but she was, albeit that gratitude was tinged with anxiety. How long could she trust a man like him, she wondered uneasily, and how long could she trust herself if he persisted in pursuing her?

It was lunchtime before she emerged from the cabin, and Pam intercepted her in the reception hall of the hotel. She had a letter with an airmail postmark in her hand, and Julie guessed it was from Adam before the other girl spoke.

'Where have you been?' she exclaimed, looking with some concern at Julie's unusually pale features. 'I thought you and Brad were going into Midland this morning. He was hanging about like a lost sheep until David went to collect the mail and took him along.'

'Oh, Pam, I forgot all about it.' Julie was dismayed. 'I'm sorry. Where is he? I must apologise.'

'He's tackling a hamburger right now,' Pam assured her lightly, pulling a wry face. 'You know nothing affects his appetite. He did come to look for you earlier with this letter, but you weren't in your cabin.'

'I was.' Ruefully Julie remembered the hammering at her door which she had taken to be the janitor. 'I—well, I had a headache,' she explained. 'I didn't feel like company.'

'And are you all right now?' Pam asked, handing her the letter addressed in Adam's neat handwriting. 'I must say you do look a little washed out. What say we have our lunch together on the terrace? A nice chef's salad with French dressing, hmm?'

Julie nodded. It was easier than thinking up an excuse, but she knew better than to suppose Pam was that easily satisfied. She read her letter while Pam went to see about the meal, but when the salad and freshly baked rolls were set before them, the older girl returned to the attack.

'You've seen Dan Prescott again, haven't you?' she remarked perceptively. 'Did he make those bruises on your arms?'

Julie crossed her arms across her chest, selfconsciously covering the revealing marks just below her shoulders with her fingers. She had been going to pass them off as the result of a fall she had had in the woods, but when Pam made so forthright a statement, she found it impossible to lie with conviction.

'He was down at the lake,' she admitted, avoiding Pam's indignant gaze. 'And that's all I'm going to say about it.'

Pam shook her head. 'The brute!' she exclaimed with feeling. 'I only hope David doesn't notice, or he'll blame me for encouraging you.'

Julie sighed. 'Pam—please, forget it. It's not important——'

'I disagree. If he thinks he can——'

'Pam, it wasn't like that.' Julie could not in all honesty allow her friend to go on imagining the worst. 'He wasn't —violent.' She paused, wishing she had never admitted anything. 'I—I bruise easily, that's all.'

'So what happened?'

Pam was all ears, ignoring completely what the other girl had said earlier, but Julie refused to discuss it. 'I'll take Brad into Midland this afternoon,' she said instead, deliberately changing the subject. 'If he still wants to go, that is.'

Pam was silent for a few minutes, and then she conceded defeat. 'Oh, he still wants to go,' she agreed offhandedly.

'He's looking forward to you treating him to one of those enormous sundaes at the ice-cream parlour. He wouldn't miss that!'

Julie forced a smile. 'I know how he feels. I shall miss them myself when I go home.'

Pam glanced quickly at her. 'You're not thinking of going home yet, though.'

Julie hesitated. 'Well—yes, actually I am. I thought perhaps—at the end of next week——'

'The end of next week!' Pam put down her fork and stared at her. 'Julie, you can't be serious! Why, we're expecting you to stay at least until August!'

Julie bent her head, resting her elbow on the edge of the table and cupping one pink-tinted cheek in her hand. 'I've loved being here, Pam, you know that,' she said uncomfortably, 'but all holidays must come to an end, and I think six weeks is enough, don't you?'

'Not really.' Pam was brusque. 'David and I have discussed this, and we feel three months might be long enough for you to get over everything you've been through. Julie, don't be in too much of a hurry to get back. Remember what you left behind.'

'I do remember, Pam——'

'What is it? Is it Adam? Is he urging you to go back? Is that what his letter says?'

'No. No. At least, not intentionally. He misses me, of course——'

'Then invite him out here,' said Pam abruptly. 'Ask him to come and stay for a couple of weeks. He has holidays, I suppose. Doesn't he?'

Julie's brow was furrowed. 'Well, yes, but——'

'But what? Isn't the Kawana good enough for him?'

'Don't be silly, Pam.' Julie sighed. 'It's not that. I—I just don't know whether he'd come. He—well, he doesn't like America.'

'This isn't America.'

'Well, North America, then.' Julie's flush deepened. 'I don't know, Pam, honestly ...'

'Invite him. See what he says. At least that way we'd get to keep you a little bit longer.'

'Oh, Pam!' Julie stretched out her hand and gripped the older girl's arm. 'You've been so kind to me ...'

'And I want to go on being kind,' declared Pam shortly. 'You know what I think? I think you're letting this—this affair with Dan Prescott frighten you away.' She paused, watching Julie's expressive face intently. 'I'm right, aren't I? That's really what decided you to go.'

'No!' Julie could not allow her to think that. 'I—well, I have to go back sooner or later.'

'Make it later,' Pam pleaded gently. 'Please, Julie. Cable Adam. Telephone him, if you like. Explain how you feel. I'm sure he'd come, if you asked him.'

The trouble was, Julie was sure he would, too, despite his reservations. If she really wanted him to come, he would make every effort to do so, but something held her back from making the call. She didn't know why, but she was loath to introduce Adam to the unsophistication of life at the Kawana Point. He wouldn't like it and he wouldn't fit in here. It wasn't that it was not luxurious enough for him; the appointments of the cabins compared very favourably with hotels back home. It was the casual attitudes he would object to, the lack of formality in manner and dress, and the easy familiarity of the other guests.

During the next couple of days she managed to avoid making any decision in the matter. When Pam asked her, she replied truthfully that she was thinking about it, and when she was with Brad she succeeded in putting it out of her mind for hours at a time.

The weather remained hot and sunny, and they swam a lot, though never from the cove where Julie had encountered Dan Prescott. It was easy to put her problems out of her mind when she was spinning across the lake at the wheel of the power-boat, or dodging the swinging sail of the dinghy, but not so easy when she retired to her cabin at night. Then she lay for hours before sleep came to claim her, waking in the morning much later than she used to with the unpleasant throbbing of an aching head.

In spite of herself she was unable to put Dan Prescott out of her mind. She could speak quite offhandedly to Pam whenever she chose to broach the subject, but in the privacy of her thoughts it was a very different matter. However she tried to avoid it, she could not forget the abandoned way she had behaved, and she burned with embarrassment every time she recalled the intimacies she had permitted him. She told herself she dreaded the thought of ever seeing him again, that if she did she would just die of shame—and yet somehow these verbal castigations did not entirely ring true.

This had been made patently obvious to her one day when two new guests arrived at the hotel. The man was tall and dark, and from behind he had looked absurdly like Dan. There was a woman with him, a slim attractive woman in her late twenties, and Julie's stomach had contracted painfully until the man had turned and she had seen he looked nothing at all like her tormentor. Nevertheless, the experience had served to make her realise that she was not as impartial as she cared to think, and she drank three beers that night in an effort to dull her over-active imagination.

By the end of that week she was no nearer making a decision, and on Saturday afternoon she rode into Midland with David and Brad on the motor launch he used to collect supplies. Leaving them at the dock, she sauntered lazily up the main shopping street, looking idly in the shop windows. There was an amazing assortment of goods for sale, and as well as the usual sports and food shops, there were dress shops and leather dealers exhibiting attractive styles for more formal occasions. Midland was not a large town, but it did have a large tourist population, and in summer there were plenty of visitors to the thirty thousand islands.

Julie was looking in the window of a book store when she became aware of someone standing behind her, and swinging round, she came face to face with him. In an open-necked navy sports shirt and the inevitable denims, he looked lean and powerful and disturbingly attractive, and Julie's limbs seemed to melt as she looked up at him. She was glad she had not succumbed to the impulse of not bothering to change before coming into town, and instead of the shorts she had been wearing, she had put on a smock dress of white printed cotton that was square-necked and sleeveless and deliciously cool.

'Hi,' she said, rather breathily, when he didn't say anything, and he inclined his head in acknowledgement. 'Small world, isn't it?'

He glanced up and down the street, and then the smoky-grey eyes returned to her slightly flushed face. 'Are you alone?'

'At the moment,' she replied, pushing her hands into the pockets of her dress. 'I came in with—with Brad and David —that's Pam's husband, but I left them down at the dock.'

'Come and have a coffee with me.'

'A coffee?' Julie licked her lips.

'A milk shake, then,' he said shortly, tucking the parcel he was carrying under his arm. 'Or a beer, if you'd rather. Just so we can talk.'

Julie drew an unsteady breath. 'I don't know . . .'

'Well, I do,' he retorted, and taking her arm, he urged her across the road and into the busy ice-cream parlour where she and Brad had spent many happy hours.

The bartender recognised him. Of course he would, thought Julie, half crossly, acknowledging his family's influence in the town, but she wondered what they thought of her, and whether this afternoon's encounter would reach his aunt's ears through the very efficient grapevine.

After installing her in one of the booths, Dan went to get their order, chatting amiably with the proprietor as he whipped up the milk and ice cream for their shakes. Milk shakes in Canada tended to be twice the size of those anywhere else, and Julie had enjoyed too many in her opinion. They were terribly fattening, but if Dan had them often, he certainly didn't show it. There wasn't any spare flesh on his bones, and she knew from experience how hard and muscular his body really was.

Remembering this brought the revealing colour back to her cheeks, and it didn't help to discover she had already attracted the interest of a group of young people seated in the opposite booth. They spoke to Dan when he came back, carrying the two shakes, and he paused to exchange a few words with them before taking his seat. Everyone seemed to know everyone else, thought Julie uncomfortably, wondering whether they thought she was his latest conquest.

'Good?' he asked, after she had swallowed a mouthful through the giant-sized straw they provided, and Julie glanced up at him through gold-tipped lashes.

'Very good, thank you,' she replied politely, and his mobile mouth slanted down rather resignedly.

'So,' he said. 'Do I take it you've forgiven me?'

'Forgiven you?' Her eyes felt glued to the glass.

'Yes.' He pushed his glass aside to rest his arms on the table, regarding her intently across its narrow width. 'Don't pretend you don't know what I mean.' He paused. 'You've given up swimming in the mornings.'

'How do you know?' The words were out before she could prevent them, and darting a look up at his set face, she knew the answer for herself.

'How do you think?' he demanded roughly, and she felt the constriction of quickening pulses. 'I want to see you again, Julie,' he went on in a low voice. 'Don't make me wait too long.'

Julie's throat closed completely. 'Dan——'

'Don't tell me no,' he warned her harshly, casting an impatient glance towards the opposite booth, and then turning back to her with smouldering eyes. 'This is a public place, and I guess you feel safe with me, but don't push it.'

'Oh, Dan, stop it!' With trembling hands she gripped the edge of the table. 'I—I can't see you again. At least, not unless you mean like this.'

'You know what I mean.'

'Yes—well, it's impossible.'

'Why?'

'Why—why, because I'm not—not free.'

'What do you mean—not free? You're not married, are you? You don't wear a ring.'

'I know, I know. But there is someone. We—we have an understanding. He trusts me.'

'Does he?' Dan's eyes regarded her with cold detachment now. 'How foolish of him!'

'That's not fair.'

'Isn't it?' He stifled an oath. 'Was it fair to act the way you did the other morning, knowing you were practically engaged to some other guy?'

Julie's mouth was dry. 'That wasn't how it was.'

'Wasn't it? How was it, then?'

Julie looked at him helplessly, her green eyes wide and troubled, and eloquently appealing. 'Dan, please . . .'

'Don't look at me like that, Julie! So pure and innocent!' He flung himself angrily back in his seat, his mouth pressed together ominously. 'So—who is this guy? Where does he live? And what's he doing letting you run around without him?'

Julie bent her head, her hair falling silkily about her ears. 'He—he lives in England,' she managed to say quietly. 'I've known him all my life.'

'So why isn't he with you?'

Julie sighed. 'Something—happened. Something I needed to get away from. Adam sent me here to—to recover.'

'Adam? That's his name?'

'Yes.'

There was silence for a few moments, and she ventured a look up at him. Dan's face was grim and as rigidly carved as stone. He was staring broodingly into the middle distance, and she wondered anxiously what was going on behind that stony façade.

As the laughing group across the aisle dispersed, Julie looked down into her rapidly flattening milkshake. That was how she felt, she thought miserably, all the lightness evaporating, leaving only the weight of her own guilt inside her. The trouble was, she didn't know which was worse— the guilt she felt towards Adam for having betrayed him, or the equally unsettling realisation that without Dan's self-control the situation could have been far more serious. Was he thinking that, too? Was he chiding himself for not having taken what she had offered when he had the chance?

Taking the straw between her lips, she drew on it rather unenthusiastically. It made a horrible sucking sound as only air was drawn into the tube, and she pushed it aside in frustration, feeling Dan's eyes watching her as she lifted her head. They were dark and disturbing, a mixture of anger and impatience, but after taking in the tremulous uncertainty of her expression they lost a little of their aggression.

'I must be crazy,' he muttered, surrendering his detachment and leaning forward to take one of her hands between both of his. 'You know, in spite of everything, I still want you.'

'No!'

Julie stared at him, half in fear, half in fascination, and he nodded his head, raising her hand to his lips, rubbing the sensitive palm with his tongue. 'Yes,' he insisted, spreading her fingers to slide his between them. 'It was good, Julie, you and me, I mean. That's how I want it to be again.'

'No!' Julie shuddered, and sat as far back in her seat as his restraining fingers would permit her. 'I—I can't. And you shouldn't ask me.'

'Why not?' His eyes were narrowed. 'What difference does it make? You're still the same person. So am I. No one else need ever know.'

Julie gasped. 'That's immoral!'

'Practical,' he corrected her coolly. 'What do you say, Julie? I want you, you want me. Why shouldn't we enjoy it?'

Julie's nails dug painfully into the formica top of the table. 'Is—is this your usual ploy, Dan? Does nothing have to stand in the way of what *you* want?'

'If you mean do I usually go for girls with complications, then the answer is no,' he retorted without rancour. 'Married women are bad news, and I avoid breaking up a good relationship.'

'How generous of you!'

Julie's sarcasm was not lost on him, but his lips only curved into a mocking smile. 'That's not to say there haven't been occasions ...' he drawled, and she felt an agonising twist of jealousy tear into her. 'So? What do you say?'

'You know what my answer is.'

'No?'

'No,' she agreed tautly.

'Oh, Julie!' His mockery fled and in its place was something far more dangerous. 'Julie,' he repeated, sliding round the banquette until his thigh was pressing against hers. 'I'm crazy about you! Don't do this to me. I need you!'

He was too intense, and her heart palpitated wildly. He was so close she could see every inch of his face, every pore and every groove, the strong line of his jaw, the slightly crooked curve of his nose, the shortness of his upper lip and the sensually fuller lower one, the blue-grey eyes, and the long dark fringe of his lashes. His skin was brown, faintly tinged around his chin with the shadow of the beard he had shaved that morning, and his hair lay thick and smooth against his head, long enough to brush his collar at the back and an irresistible temptation to her fingers. His open shirt revealed the upper half of his chest with its light covering of dark hair, and she could remember only too well the feel of his skin against hers. He was right, she thought in consternation, she did want him. And the knowledge horrified her.

His arm was along the seat behind her, his hand closing possessively over her bare shoulder, and her knees shook. When his fingers probed beneath the strap of her dress, however, she knew she could stand no more.

'Dan, don't!' she got out chokingly, unable to look at him but instilling her voice with the urgency of her feelings. 'I— I have to go. David's waiting for me——'

Her words died beneath his mouth, his parted lips covering hers and taking a moist possession. The pressure he exerted was light, but Julie felt her senses swimming.

The sound of voices penetrated her sexually-induced inertia, voices she recognised, and she managed to drag herself away from Dan just in time as David and his son came to occupy the opposite booth.

'Hey, Julie!'

It was Brad who saw her first as his father was about to go to the bar, and she prayed she did not look as disconcerted as she felt. With Dan's fingers still imprisoning her wrist under cover of the table top, and his lazy eyes upon her, she found it incredibly difficult to act normally and had to force herself to listen to what the boy was saying.

'Hi, Mr Prescott.' Thankfully Brad had switched his attention to her companion, and David paused to greet the other man.

'I didn't know we'd find you here, Julie,' he said, and she

wondered if she imagined the note of disapproval in his voice. 'I thought you had some shopping to do.'

There was no mistake. David was not pleased, and Julie could hardly blame him. After all, he had warned her about Dan Prescott, and he also knew of the loyalty she owed to Adam.

'I was looking in shop windows when—when I bumped into—into Mr Prescott,' she volunteered. 'We—er—I was just leaving.'

'Oh, don't go!' Brad looked disappointed. 'Say, when are you going to show me the yacht, Mr Prescott. You haven't forgotten, have you?'

'No, I haven't forgotten, Brad,' Dan assured him good-humouredly, as the boy's father uttered a word of reproval. 'It's okay, Mr Galloway, honestly. I know what it's like when people make promises they don't keep.' He had to release Julie's wrist to slide out of the booth, and while she ran a nervous hand over her hair he continued: 'I'll come by one afternoon next week, and we'll go for a sail. How would that suit you?'

'Really, Mr Prescott, that's not necessary,' David began, stung by his conscience, but Dan dismissed his objections.

'It's okay, Mr Galloway,' he assured him, with a grin, and transferring his attention to the boy added: 'It's a date. See you, Brad.'

'See you, Mr Prescott,' Brad agreed excitedly, and Julie emerged from the ice-cream parlour with the uneasy feeling that she held his happiness in the palm of her hand.

The sunlight was brilliant after the dimness of the booth, and as she shaded her eyes Dan slipped a possessive hand about her waist. 'Walk with me,' he said, and she had no choice but to accompany him down the steeply sloping street to the dock.

It was quite an experience walking with him. He knew nearly half the people they passed, and their close proximity was not lost on speculatively probing eyes. But Dan seemed unperturbed, and exchanged a word here and there without any apparent embarrassment.

'You can leave me here,' Julie said at last, after they had crossed the railway line and were standing on the dazzling strip of concrete fronting the dock. 'That's David's launch. I'll wait for them on board.'

'Let me take you home,' Dan suggested casually. 'I came on the Honda, and it'll be much cooler riding through the woods.'

And much more dangerous, added Julie silently, shaking her head. 'I don't think so.'

Dan sighed, resting one hand on each of her shoulders, looking down at her in mild irritation. 'You're not going to start all over, are you?' he protested. 'You know it's only a matter of time before—well, let's agree that we attract one another, and where's the harm in a holiday relationship anyway?'

'Are you on holiday?' Julie asked suspiciously.

'Sort of.'

'What's that supposed to mean?'

Dan grinned. 'I'm supposed to be recuperating.'

Julie could not prevent the twinge of anxiety that gripped her. 'Have you been ill?'

'Appendicitis,' he explained dryly. 'D'you want to see my scar?'

'No!' Julie flushed, and then realising he was teasing her, turned away. 'I'd better go ...'

His hands on her waist prevented her from doing so, and presently she felt his body close behind her. 'When am I going to see you again?' he demanded urgently. 'Tonight? Tomorrow? Promise me you'll come down to the lake in the morning and I'll let you go.'

Julie drew a deep breath. 'And what about your family? Do they know what you're doing? Do they know about me?'

He was silent for a few moments, and then he said quietly: 'Drew does.'

'Your cousin?'

'Yes.'

'And your aunt and uncle?' Julie couldn't prevent herself from going on even though it was like sticking a knife in herself and twisting the blade. 'Pam told me about the Leytons—about your family.'

Dan took her arms and turned her to face him. 'So?'

'So——' Julie pressed her lips together for a moment to prevent them from trembling, 'they don't know about me, do they? I'm nothing to them, just another of Dan's little——'

'Stop it!'

He cut into her words angrily, but she was committed to destroying their relationship and she had to continue.

'They wouldn't approve of our association, would they? I mean—a suicide's daughter and a banker's son! It's just not on, is it? And that's the way it is with you, too, isn't it? All you want from me is an affair. A holiday relationship, as you said. Well, I don't have—affairs, Mr Prescott. So you'd better save yourself for someone who does!'

'You don't know what you're talking about,' he said coldly, but his hands had dropped to his sides, and with a little shiver she turned and walked away—and he let her.

CHAPTER FOUR

THE Boeing 747 landed at Toronto's international airport just before six o'clock, but Julie had to wait another half hour for Adam to get his baggage and go through customs before he was free to walk through to the reception hall. He was among the first to emerge, a porter carrying his suitcase and the briefcase without which he went nowhere, and he looked so dear and familiar that Julie practically threw herself into his waiting arms. His gentle embrace was so soothing after the hectic emotions she had been suppressing, and tears came to her eyes as he drew back to look at her.

'Did you miss me?' he teased, though his shrewd gaze was apt to see more than she either knew or wanted. 'Are you all right? You look a little feverish to me. I thought you said that this climate agreed with you.'

'I did. It does.' Julie urged him impatiently towards the elevators. 'Come along. The car's parked on the sixth level. We can talk after we've left the airport.'

Adam obediently followed her, taking his cases from the porter and thanking him for his trouble. Then they squeezed into the metal elevator and shared the ride with a dozen others all bent on the same purpose.

The traffic was brisk as they joined the highway, but for once Adam relaxed in his seat beside her. Perhaps the journey had tired him, Julie thought, for usually he objected to her taking the wheel when he was in the car. He did look a little pale, but perhaps that was because she was used to David's weathered appearance, and most of the men she knew were tanned. He seemed smaller, too, his build slimmer, his fair hair lighter and thinner—but again, the larger country seemed to breed larger men, and she had

56

been here more than six weeks ...

'Did you have a good journey?' she asked, as the traffic began to thin, banishing the unwilling thoughts of Dan Prescott that persistently troubled her. 'At least the flight was on time. I've only been waiting about forty-five minutes.'

'Forty-five minutes!' Adam sounded appalled. 'Why didn't you just book me into an hotel, and let me take a cab into the city?'

'Because I wanted to meet you,' declared Julie swiftly. 'You came here because of me. The least I could do——'

'My dear girl, I came because you needed me,' Adam retorted dryly. 'I've missed you, and when you telephoned I was concerned about you.'

Julie pressed her lips together. 'But you needn't have come out here.'

'I wanted to,' exclaimed Adam forcefully. 'You sounded so—so strung up on the phone. I realised you were not fit to make the journey home alone, so I decided to accept the Galloway's invitation to spend a few days at Georgian Bay.'

'Oh, Adam ...' She glanced at him affectionately. 'You know you'll hate it. The great outdoors is not really your scene, is it?'

Adam chuckled. 'Perhaps not. If what you're wearing is a sample of the current fashion, I'm going to be hopelessly out of place.'

Julie laughed too, relaxing for the first time in days, though her mirth was short-lived. She had forgotten Adam's aversion to jeans and in her haste to get to the airport in plenty of time, she had not bothered to change.

'Nobody cares what you wear at Kawana Point,' she told him, sustaining her smile with difficulty. 'But they're very nice, and very friendly, and I know they'll make you welcome.'

Adam nodded. 'But I gather they don't dress for dinner,' he remarked wryly, and she shook her head. 'So I won't be needing my dinner jacket, will I? Unless you and I spend some time in Toronto before going home.'

Julie's expression grew a little doubtful, and she guessed he could sense her uncertainty. 'Perhaps,' she murmured, wishing she had defied him and taken the London flight. 'We'll see.'

It was a long drive to Midland and after leaving the outskirts of the city behind they passed through miles and miles of open land, not unlike England but bigger and flatter. The trees were sparser too, and the houses they saw seemed remote from their neighbours.

'How can anyone live so far from any larger communities?' asked Adam in dismay. 'I hope we're not going to be staying miles from anywhere. You know I like the daily papers, and somewhere to buy my tobacco.'

Julie sighed. 'Well, the Kawana is off the beaten track,' she confessed, 'but I warned you——'

'How far off the beaten track?' he cut in resignedly, and she shrugged.

'David has a motor launch. It takes about thirty minutes to get into Midland.'

'And Midland is what?'

'The nearest town. It's quite a pleasant place. It has hotels, and a movie theatre, and plenty of restaurants. I like it.'

Adam's note was thoughtful. 'Oh, well, I suppose I can put up with it for a few days,' he conceded. 'But going back to nature doesn't appear to have done you a lot of good.'

'Adam, the Kawana Point is not "going back to nature",' she protested, turning to give him a half impatient look. 'It's a modern, comfortable hotel. The food is out of this world!'

'Well, you do appear to have put on a little weight,' Adam agreed dryly. 'Or perhaps it's just those clothes you're wearing. Where did you get that shirt? Isn't that what pregnant mothers wear?'

Julie contained her indignation. 'It's a smock,' she told

him patiently. 'I suppose pregnant mothers do wear them, but they also happen to be very cool and very comfortable.'

'But not very fashionable,' put in Adam shortly, and she decided not to argue. 'So,' he added, when it became obvious she was not going to continue, 'why did you want to come home so abruptly? I thought you were enjoying your stay.'

'I was. I am.' Julie caught her lower lip between her teeth. 'Only—well, I just wanted to come home, that's all. Homesickness, I guess.'

'You guess?' Adam's tone indicated his opinion of the Americanism. 'And why did you suddenly get homesick? It doesn't appear to have worried you up until now?'

Julie shrugged. 'I suppose I missed you.'

'Well, thank you.' His response was ironic. 'Is that all?'

'What else could there be?'

'You tell me.'

Julie hesitated. 'Did you—did you clear everything up?'

'About your father's estate? Of course. There wasn't much left to do, as you know. You handled most of that before you came away.'

Julie nodded. 'I—is—is Mrs Collins still living at the house?'

'Naturally. Until you decide to sell, she'll continue to do so.'

Julie's fingers tightened on the wheel. 'Would—would he really have gone to prison?'

'Julie, your father knew there was every chance. He wanted to save you that, so he took his own life. That's all that needs to be said. He wrote his own epitaph.'

'If only I'd known him better,' she sighed wistfully. 'I saw more of you than I did of him.'

'Julie, after your mother died——'

'I know.' She sighed again. 'Well, it's over, as you say. Nothing I say or do can bring him back.'

'No.' But Adam's voice was gentle now. 'Let's talk about

other things. What have you been doing since you came here? I would imagine there's plenty of scope for swimming and sailing, that sort of thing.'

'There is.' Julie closed her mind against Dan's image. 'Brad—that's Pam and David's son—he's been trying to teach me to water-ski. He's quite good at it, but I'm just a mess!'

'Water-skiing?' Adam grimaced. 'You mean—in wet-suits and the like?'

'Actually, no. Just bathing suits,' said Julie ruefully. 'It stings like mad when you do a belly-flop!'

'But the lake must be freezing when you get out from the shore,' Adam protested, and Julie nodded in agreement.

'It is. But you get used to it. And when it's hot . . .'

Adam looked as if the whole idea appalled him, and she allowed the topic to lapse. She couldn't expect Adam to appreciate such youthful pursuits. He was a lot older, after all, and she couldn't ever remember him liking to take his clothes off. She remembered a holiday she had had with him and her father at a villa in the South of France. Her father had spent more time in the pool than Adam had, and he had been at least ten years older.

Shrugging, she applied her attention to her driving, and it was Adam who broke the uneasy silence that had fallen. 'Are there any other hotels within reach of Kawana?' he asked. 'Do people live around the lake? Are there villages, settlements?'

'They're mostly holiday homes,' Julie replied a little tightly. 'There aren't any villages, as such, Adam. There are towns, and there are small towns. That's it.'

'Hmm.' Adam was thoughtful. 'But what about the people who live in these holiday homes? Who are they?'

'I don't know, do I?' Julie gave an impatient shrug. 'Do you want to stop for a meal? There's a small town up ahead where we could have some dinner, if you like.'

Adam glanced sideways at her, then he made a negative

gesture. 'I don't think so, thanks all the same. You know what it's like on that transatlantic flight—they ply you with food and drink from the minute you get on board. And besides, my metabolism keeps telling me it's after midnight.' He paused. 'Are there many guests at the hotel?'

Julie's fingers tightened over the wheel. 'About a dozen,' she answered offhandedly. 'What film did they show coming over? Did you go and see that French film we were discussing before I came away? I'm probably hopelessly out of touch with everything.'

Once again Adam subjected her to a probing stare, and then, shifting more comfortably in his seat, he replied to her questions, talking about the movie they had shown on the flight, describing the various French and Italian films that were presently playing in London. For a while, he succeeded in distracting Julie's mind from everything else, and her knuckles ceased to show through the creamy brown skin.

Inevitably, however, the conversation shifted back to their destination, and Julie tried to speak casually when she described an ordinary day at the hotel.

'How long do people stay?' enquired Adam curiously, and she replied that occasionally guests had lingered for three and four weeks at a time.

'There's plenty to do, if you like fishing and sailing,' she protested, in response to Adam's grunt of dismay. 'It's a sportsman's paradise, and the scenery is beautiful!'

'Hmm. But I imagine most people commute at weekends only,' Adam averred. 'These holiday homes you mentioned —I doubt if they're in use all the time. I knew a chap from New York once who had a cabin in the Adirondacks. I suppose this is a similar retreat.'

Why had Adam to mention New York? Julie asked herself despairingly. New York was synonymous with all the things she wanted to forget, and the fact that Dan lived there was prime among them. It was useless to pretend she could forget about him here. Until she got away she would always feel this hollow emptiness every time she let some casual association remind her of the time they had spent together.

'Have you got to know any of the guests personally?'

Adam's query brought her back to the present, but the look she cast his way revealed the blankness in her eyes. 'I—oh, no. No,' she got out jerkily, as her brain comprehended his question. 'I mean, they're usually couples, or families—and I've spent most of my time with the Galloways.'

'I see.' Adam pulled his pipe out of his pocket and began to examine the bowl. 'So who has upset you, Julie? Someone working at the hotel, perhaps? Or David Galloway himself?'

If Julie had not had to concentrate on her driving she might easily have burst into tears at that moment. It was humiliating to feel one was so transparent, and while she applauded his perception, she could not forgive his timing.

'I don't know what you mean,' she lied, keeping her eyes glued to the road ahead. 'No one's upset me, least of all David! If you knew him, you wouldn't suggest such a thing.'

'All right.' Adam tamped the tobacco in his pipe, and then applied his lighter to the bowl. 'My apologies to Galloway, but someone's upset you, and I'd like to know who it is before we get there.'

'Adam!' Julie glanced indignantly at him. 'I've told you——'

'I know what you've told me, Julie,' he replied calmly, slipping his lighter back into his pocket and drawing comfortably on the burning tobacco. 'But I also know that you're more highly strung now than you were before you went away, and that's not like you at all.'

'You're imagining things.' Julie licked her suddenly dry lips. 'I'm just a little fed-up, that's all. Secondary reaction, I guess. Losing one's father so suddenly and in such a way isn't easy to swallow.'

'I know that.' Adam's tone was compassionate. 'But you were over the worst of it Julie. Believe me, you were on the mend when you left England. That was why I let you come here, because I thought this holiday would complete the cure. You've never been a particularly neurotic girl. You're emotional, I know that, but not abnormally so. Now I come here to find you're on edge and impatient, answering my questions as if I was subjecting you to an inquisition. You're nervous, and touchy. Not like my Julie at all. And I mean to know why.'

'Oh, Adam ...'

'Don't look at me like that. I know what I'm talking about, Julie. I know you too well to be deceived. Now, something's happened, hasn't it? Are you going to tell me? Or do I have to find out for myself?'

Julie heaved a heavy sigh. She didn't know what to do. Adam did know her well, it was true, none better, but this was something outside the bonds of their relationship. Indeed, it could destroy their relationship once and for all, and she didn't want that.

'Adam,' she said at last, 'it's nothing, *really*.' She paused. 'If I admit that something did happen, something that did upset me, will you just let it go? Please?'

Adam was silent for a few minutes, drawing on his pipe, and then he said quietly: 'Are you sure *you* want to let it go, Julie? Isn't that what all this is about? Wanting to come home? Your uncertainty? Wouldn't it be simpler if you were completely honest with yourself?'

'But I am being,' she protested, taking her attention from the road to stare at him appealingly. 'Honestly, Adam, it—it wasn't important. And it's all over. Over!'

'Really?'

'Yes, really.' She paused, realising he deserved something more. 'It wasn't—well, like you think. That is, there was never any question of—of it being serious. It was just a brief interlude. Nothing happened, Adam. Nothing at all.'

He frowned. 'I'm beginning to see a little light here. It was someone who stayed at the hotel, wasn't it? Someone the Galloways know about. And that's why you're on edge, why you didn't want me to come here. Because you were afraid they might tell me.'

Julie opened her mouth to deny this, and then closed it again. How much simpler it would be if Adam thought that, she conceded, ignoring the pangs of her conscience. If he imagined it had been a brief holiday romance with someone who had now left the area, she might conceivably be able to relax.

When she didn't say anything for so long, Adam nodded and then stretched out a hand to grip her knee for a moment. 'You don't have to say anything, Julie,' he said quietly, making her feel even worse. 'You're young—and beautiful. It's natural that young men should be attracted to you. And I'm not going to blame you if you enjoyed the experience. Perhaps it's served a useful purpose after all. It's brought us together again, and that's what matters, isn't it?'

Julie forced a smile and covered his hand with one of hers for a moment. If only Adam wasn't so understanding, she thought, taking a determined grip upon her emotions. She might have felt better if he had ranted and raved and blown his top. As it was, she felt a little like a child who has stolen a handful of sticky candy, who knows he has done wrong, and isn't punished for it. The guilt was not expunged, it remained.

David and Brad were waiting for them at Midland, and Julie handed over the reins of responsibility with some relief. The car, an old Pontiac, was left at the wharf, and they all climbed aboard the motor launch.

'Did you have a good trip, Mr Price?' David enquired politely, as he stowed the luggage, but Brad forestalled any reply by jumping in with his own exciting news.

'He came, Julie, he came!' he exclaimed, almost jumping up and down in his enthusiasm, and the boat rocked alarmingly. 'Mr Prescott, Dan! He said I could call him that,' he added proudly. 'When we were out on the lake.'

Julie's legs gave out on her and she sank down weakly beside Adam, hoping he would imagine her unsteadiness was due to the upheaval of the boat. David, aware of her suddenly pale face, chastised his son roundly for almost overturning the launch, and then repeated his question to Adam as if nothing more important had happened.

'He took me out on the yacht,' Brad persisted, talking over Adam's moderate reply. 'D'you know what it's called? The yacht, I mean? *Spirit of Atlantis*! Isn't that a terrific name?'

'Brad, will you be quiet?' His father's hand upon his shoulder was a distinct warning, and the boy pulled a sulky face as he subsided on to the engine housing. 'I'm sorry, Mr Price, my son thinks there's nothing more important than sailing at the moment.'

'That's all right.' Adam crossed his legs, the polished toe of his shoe in direct contrast to David's canvas sneakers. 'I know what boys are like. I have two nephews myself.'

David smiled his understanding, but the look he cast in Julie's direction was more constrained, and catching his eyes upon her, she was puzzled by his expression. He looked both angry and frustrated, but when she arched her brows in anxious enquiry he turned abruptly away, the shake of his head almost imperceptible.

For her part, Julie was desperately trying to regain her self-control. Brad's words had certainly robbed her of the composure she had achieved during the journey from the airport, and her mind throbbed with unanswered questions. Why had Dan come to the hotel? Had it only been to take Brad out? Had he expected to see her? Or was he merely keeping the promise he had made to the boy?

Whatever the answers to these questions, one thing was certain. He would now know all about Adam. Brad was too much of a chatterbox not to have related where Julie was and why, and surely that would curtail any further intentions Dan might have had of continuing their unsatisfactory association. It was four days since that awful scene on the wharf, after all, and Julie had succeeded in convincing herself that she was never likely to see him again. Apart from anything else, the callous way she had thrown her father's suicide at him would have deterred the most ardent suitor, and Dan certainly was not that.

It was a beautiful evening, the sky hazing from lemon yellow to deepest purple, and Julie made an effort to point out the places of interest to Adam. She indicated the deserted crescent of Snake Island and the tangled mass of islands beyond, and then explained that the Kawana Point Hotel was situated at the mouth of one of the many bays that intersected the coastline.

'It's like an inland sea,' exclaimed Adam, in reluctant admiration. 'One could almost imagine getting lost on such an enormous expanse of water.'

'You can get lost among the islands unless you know the channels,' put in Brad, with a hasty glance at his father. 'You can run aground, and Mr Prescott says——'

'That will do, Brad.' Once again, David interrupted him, and Julie couldn't prevent the wave of sympathy she felt towards the boy even if his words did fill her with apprehension. When he looked indignantly in her direction, she gave him a sympathetic smile, and then half wished she hadn't when he scrambled over Adam's suitcase and came to join her.

Adam was talking to David, asking about the kind of fishing that was available in the area, and Brad took the opportunity to speak to Julie alone. 'You should have been there,' he exclaimed, his eyes wide and excited, and she had

no need to ask to what he was referring. 'She's a beauty—
the yacht, I mean. There are three cabins and three bath-
rooms—heads, I should say,' he grinned, glancing surreptitiously over his shoulder to make sure his father wasn't
listening, 'and it can do nearly thirty knots!'

Julie tried to assume an interest she was far from feeling.
'Really?' she asked, apparently impressed. 'You'll have
something to tell your friends when you get back to school.'

'Gosh, yes.' Brad nodded reminiscently. 'He's nice, Mr
Prescott, isn't he? He let me take the wheel. Dad wouldn't
believe me when I told him, but Mr Prescott doesn't worry
about things like that.' He paused. 'He likes you, Julie. He
said so. He asked where you were, and I told him. That's
all right, isn't it?'

'Of course.' Julie drew an uneven breath. 'Why not?'

Brad shrugged. 'I don't know.' He cast another doubtful
look in his father's direction. 'Dad said you wouldn't be
interested in anything Mr Prescott had to say. Not now
that your boy-friend's here.' He frowned. 'Is Mr Price
your boy-friend, Julie. He looks—old!'

'He's only thirty-eight, Brad,' she retorted impatiently,
annoyed to find that she could resent David's assumption
even so. 'About the same age as your father.'

'I know, but Dad's been married for years and years!'

'I doubt if your mother would appreciate your senti-
ments,' remarked Julie dryly, but Brad was unrepentant.

'Anyway, Mr Prescott—*Dan*—said that he expected he'd
be seeing you again.' He moved his shoulders offhandedly.
'Only don't tell Dad I told you.'

CHAPTER FIVE

THE invitation came at lunchtime the following day. A man in the uniform of a chauffeur delivered it, arriving aboard a highly-powered cruiser and insisting that he had been instructed to wait for a reply.

Julie saw the man as she and Adam sat at their table in the dining room, and although she had no reason to suspect who he was or why he was here, she could not prevent the tingle of apprehension that rippled along her spine when Pam carried the envelope into the restaurant. She looked uncomfortable as she approached them, and Julie, used to her casual, easy-going manner, was alarmed.

'I'm sorry to disturb you,' she offered apologetically, indicating the envelope in her hand. 'But he——' she glanced over her shoulder, 'he insisted on waiting for a reply.'

'What is it?' Julie tried to sound unconcerned and failed. 'Not bad news, I hope.'

'Not exactly.' Pam was hesitant, and Adam gave her an encouraging smile.

'I'm sure it can't be anything too terrible, Pamela,' he assured her gently. 'The gentleman's not a policeman, is he?'

'Heavens, no!' Pam shook her head and gave a short laugh, and Julie wished she would simply tell them what it was and get it over with. 'It's from—from the Leytons, Julie.'

She gave the younger girl the envelope, and Julie lifted the thick parchment flap with unsteady fingers. Inside was a card, a single card, the edge delicately serrated and tinted a palest rose. It was from Anthea Leyton, inviting Mr and

68

Mrs David Galloway and their two guests, Mr Adam Price and Miss Julie Osbourne, to a barbecue they were holding that evening at Forest Bay.

Julie said nothing. She couldn't. She merely handed the card to Adam and while he read it, exchanged a look of shaken bewilderment with Pam. The other girl lifted her shoulders in helpless acquiescence and looked at Adam as he spoke.

'Is something wrong with this invitation?' he asked, raising his eyebrows. 'It seems eminently satisfactory to me. Who are these people? Do you know them? Well, of course, you must do, if they're inviting us to dinner.'

Pam sighed. 'I—we—I haven't actually met—Mrs Leyton,' she admitted. 'I—er—I've met her nephew.' She glanced appealingly towards Julie. 'You remember Dan Prescott, don't you, Julie? He came to the hotel a couple of weeks ago.'

'Yes.' Julie's mouth was dry, but she managed to articulate. 'I remember. I—are you—going to accept?'

'Are you?' Pam's meaning was clear, and Julie could only move her shoulders in helpless indecision.

'Prescott, Prescott?' Adam was saying thoughtfully. 'Where have I heard that name before? Oh, yes, it was your son, Pamela. Didn't he say that Mr Prescott had taken him out on his yacht?'

'That's right.' Pam couldn't deny it. 'He came yesterday, Julie. After you'd gone to the airport to meet Adam.'

Meeting Pam's eyes as she said this, Julie felt the tide of embarrassment sweeping up her cheeks. She had gone out of her way to avoid discussing the previous day's events with Pam, but now it seemed it was impossible after all.

'Well,' Adam was speaking again, 'I must say it's very civil of them to invite us. Are they residents in the area?'

Pam hesitated, then she said: 'Forest Bay is the Leytons' summer residence. Mrs Leyton is Lionel Prescott's sister. You may have heard of the Scott National Bank?'

'*That* Lionel Prescott?' Adam was impressed.

'Yes.' It was Julie who answered him, giving Pam an impatient look. 'I expect it's just a—a gesture. People like that do those sort of things.'

'I think we should accept.' Pam made her statement almost belligerently. 'After all, we are their tenants, and I'd hate to offend them.'

Julie stared at her friend incredulously. Pam didn't really believe that, any more than she believed the invitation was genuine. Dan was behind this, it was at his instigation they had been invited—but what his game was she didn't dare to think.

'Yes, I agree.' Adam's words broke into her agitated thoughts. 'It sounds delightful, and it will give me a chance to wear my dinner jacket after all, eh, Julie?'

'What?' Julie was still looking accusingly at Pam, and it was difficult to concentrate on what Adam was saying.

'I said—I'll be able to use my dinner jacket,' he repeated, and then turning to Pam added, rather doubtfully: 'A dinner jacket will be in order, won't it?'

Pam assured him that it would, and then retrieving the invitation card from Julie's unresisting fingers, she went to give their reply to the messenger. Julie, unable to continue with her lunch in her present state, excused herself on the pretext of fetching a handkerchief, but after the man had departed she followed her friend into the small office behind the reception desk.

'And what do you think David's going to say?' she demanded, closing the door behind her so that their conversation should not be overheard. 'You know how he feels about the Leytons—and Dan Prescott, for that matter!'

Pam shrugged, perching on the corner of the desk and re-reading the card with annoying deliberation. 'He can't refuse now, can he?' she responded without heat. 'And I've always wanted to see the inside of that place.'

Julie did not deign to ask what place. She merely stood

there, pressing her lips together, waiting for Pam to say something to ease her raw emotions.

After a few moments Pam looked up and seeing her tension, adopted a conciliatory tone. 'Don't look like that, Julie,' she exclaimed. 'It'll be fun, you'll see. And it's not as if you're going alone. Adam will be with you, and Dan Prescott can hardly come between you two, can he?'

Julie stared at her for a few minutes more, then her tension seemed to snap and her shoulders sagged. 'Why is he doing this, Pam?' she groaned, sinking down on to the chair beside the door, and her friend regarded her compassionately.

'I think he's more serious than you think,' she admitted, unwillingly. 'Wait and see. Maybe the invitation's as innocuous as it seems.'

'You don't believe that.' Julie sniffed, looking up at her.

'No.' Pam was honest. 'But you shouldn't jump to conclusions.'

'Pam, I'm going to marry Adam!'

'I'm not denying it, am I?'

'No,' Julie conceded with a sigh. 'But Dan Prescott doesn't care about that. He doesn't care about anybody but himself. He practically told me there had been other women ... *married* women ...'

Pam sighed. 'Well, I don't know of any.' She grimaced. 'Chance would be a fine thing!'

'Pam!'

'Well!' The other girl was unrepentant. 'He is a dish, isn't he? It would be worth it just for the experience.'

Julie shook her head. 'You're crazy!'

'And you're far too serious for a girl of your age. Take it easy, Julie! Don't worry. Just think—in less than two weeks you'll be back in England, and all this will have faded from your mind.'

Julie wished she could feel as confident. The trouble was she was finding it increasingly difficult to keep Dan's image out of her thoughts, and somehow she doubted even a distance of some three and a half thousand miles would make the slightest difference. She had only to close her eyes to find his face imprinted on her lids, his grey eyes crinkling at the corners, his mouth lifted in that lazy sensuous smile.

As expected, David objected to Pam's arbitrary acceptance of the invitation, but he was on a fishing trip with two of the guests from the hotel, and by the time he returned it was too late to do anything about it. Besides, as his wife argued, they had a very satisfactory staff, and it was time they had a night out together.

Julie, for her part, had mixed feelings. Despite her fears, she could not deny the purely physical excitement she experienced every time she thought of seeing Dan again, and in consequence she took longer than she should choosing what to wear.

Eventually she decided on a simple black evening gown she had stuffed into her case all those weeks ago in England. She had not expected to need it, but it was easy to pack and crease-resistant, and its plain lines were both flattering and elegant. Narrow straps tied on her shoulders above a draped bodice that was cut almost to the waist at the back and fell in soft folds to a few inches above her ankle. It was made of a silky acrylic fibre that clung where it touched, and it accentuated the creamy tan she had acquired. With her hair loose about her shoulders, she knew she would not disappoint Adam, and she felt a little more prepared to face the Leytons.

They used the launch to reach the party, crossing the bay and rounding the promontory to where the Leytons' summer residence was situated. It was a warm evening, and not yet dark as David steered the small craft across the water, and Pam exchanged a conspiratorial smile with Julie.

'You look gorgeous,' she said, looking down ruefully at

her own flower-printed cotton. 'I wish I was twelve pounds lighter. I'd wear something sexy too.'

Julie looked a little apprehensive at that. 'Do you think it is—too sexy, I mean?' she asked anxiously. 'I don't want anyone to——'

'No, of course not!' Pam overrode her protest with an envious grimace. 'Honestly, Julie, you look lovely. Doesn't she, Adam?' She turned to the man who was standing beside David at the wheel. 'Doesn't Julie look stunning?'

'Stunning,' Adam echoed, with an indulgent squeeze of her arm. 'But then she always does,' he added, for her ears only, and she wondered why Adam's compliments always sounded slightly patronising.

There were several boats moored at the breakwater that jutted into the lake below the Leytons' house, some of them as opulently luxuriant as Brad had described the Leytons' yacht to be. A planked jetty was connected to the gardens of the house by a flight of wooden steps, and the whole landing area was illuminated by coloured lights concealed inside swinging Japanese lanterns. The sound of music and laughter and muted voices drifted over the water, and Julie felt her nerves tightening as David tossed the painter on to the jetty and vaulted out after it.

'I'm petrified,' Pam confessed, as she gathered her skirts ready to go ashore, and her husband gave her an aggravated look.

'Don't blame me!' he declared pointedly, uncomfortable in his formal clothes, and his wife pulled a face at him as a uniformed steward came to assist him.

'Let me do that for you, sir,' he insisted, fastening the rope quickly and expertly before offering a hand to each of the girls in turn, and David grumbled gruffly to himself as they all walked along the jetty.

Pam and David climbed the steps first and Julie felt her heart hammering in her chest as she and Adam followed them. Now that she was here, she was convinced she ought not to have come, and her hand tightened uncontrollably on Adam's sleeve.

Their hosts were waiting to greet them, and Julie didn't know whether to feel relieved or apprehensive that Dan was not with them. There was no sign of him, and her tongue came to moisten her dry lips as she took in the animated scene. There was so much to see and absorb, and the gardens of the house seemed full of people in every style and mode of dress, from the inevitable denims to evening gowns and white tuxedos. There were so many colours, so much variety, and the white-coated waiters threading among the guests carrying trays of champagne and canapés seemed impervious to the carelessly-placed hands and feet that impeded their progress. Beyond the manicured lawns she could see a flower-filled patio and buffet tables, and an enormous charcoal grill smouldering under a huge sirloin of beef.

Many curious eyes had turned in their direction as Maxwell Leyton took over the introductions. He and David had met before, although not under these circumstances, and he thanked them all politely for coming before turning to his wife.

Anthea Leyton was one of the most beautiful women Julie had ever seen. She was dark, like her nephew, with the same misty grey eyes and curling lashes, and her gown of rose-printed silk complemented her olive skin. She wore diamonds in her ears and at her throat, and the chunky bracelet around her wrist was obviously worth a small fortune, but if her appearance was attractive, her manner was not. Her acknowledgement of the Galloways had hardly been polite, and now she turned to Julie with a vaguely speculative hostility.

'So you're Julie,' she said, and the way she said it was hardly flattering. 'My nephew has mentioned you, but I was curious to meet you for myself.'

'Yes?'

Julie's heart seemed to stop and then start again, labouring under the effort. What was this woman trying to say? That she had been responsible for issuing the invitations? That Dan had had nothing to do with it?

'I believe you're English, aren't you?' she continued, apparently unaware of Julie's faltering expression. 'You must tell me what you think of our small country.'

Julie made a helpless gesture, and to her relief Anthea turned her attention to Adam. 'Good evening, Mr Price. I hope you'll enjoy your evening.'

'I'm sure I shall,' he assured her politely, and for once Julie was glad of his very English self-possession, although she wondered what he had made of Anthea's oblique comments. 'This is a beautiful place you have here, Mrs Leyton. An oasis of sophistication for an old epicurean like me.'

Anthea looked as if she wasn't sure whether or not to take him seriously, but at least his remarks had taken the onus off Julie. It gave her the opportunity to scan the crowd once again, but it was impossible to distinguish one tall man among so many. She tried to tell herself she was glad he wasn't around, that she ought to be grateful to Anthea for confirming what she had suspected, and then, just as Adam was leading her away to where Pam and David were waiting, a lazily familiar voice said: 'Hi.'

Julie felt as if someone had just delivered a blow to her solar plexis, and her hand in Adam's arm fell abruptly away. Dan was standing right behind them, casually dressed in light blue trousers and a cream silk open-necked shirt, the only sign of affluence the dark blue velvet jacket that accentuated the width of his shoulders.

'Glad you could make it,' he remarked, giving Adam a swift appraisal before seeking Julie's heated features. 'I'm sorry I wasn't here to meet you, but my aunt insists on utilising every available hand.'

'Er—this is Dan Prescott, Adam,' Julie managed to say hastily. 'Adam Price, Dan.'

'How do you do, Mr Prescott.'

Adam held out his hand and Dan shook it, moving between them to do so, successfully isolating Julie on his right. Then he grinned at Pam and exchanged a word with David before suggesting that he introduced them to some of the other guests.

It seemed the most natural thing in the world that he should walk between them, though Julie sensed Adam's dissatisfaction with the arrangement. However, with Pam and David right beside him he could hardly offer any objection, but Julie guessed he would have more to say later.

Most of the guests acknowledged Dan's introductions with only minor interest. Several of the women gave Julie a critical look and once or twice she sensed the hostility she had felt from Anthea, but for the most part, people were bent on enjoying themselves, and the freely flowing alcohol had oiled the stiffest bearing. There was the hum of conversation, the outburst of laughter, and the musical sounds from the loudspeakers to ensure that no awkward silences occurred. Some of the younger guests were even dancing on the patio, and with darkness falling across the lake the whole scene had the appearance of a stage set.

'Well? What do you think?' Dan murmured in an undertone, bending his head towards Julie as if in answer to something she had said, and she smelt the clean fragrance of his aftershave. 'Did Aunt Anthea make you welcome, or did she give one of her famous impressions of Lucrezia Borgia?'

Julie couldn't say anything in reply, but a faint smile touched her lips as she looked away. He was the same Dan, in spite of everything, she thought, but she wished he would not make it so hard for her.

Glasses of champagne were offered, and Julie buried her nose in the bubbling liquid. Adam was talking to David and a man on his left, who apparently drove formula one racing cars, and Pam wrinkled her nose above the delicate rim of her glass.

'Nectar,' she mouthed, rolling her eyes expressively, and Julie wished she could feel as uninhibited as her friend.

Dan swallowed his champagne without reverence and slipped his fingers around Julie's wrist, twisting it behind his back. 'Dance with me,' he said, all the humour gone from his face, and she felt the familiar pull of her senses as his thumb massaged her palm.

'I—I can't,' she murmured, hoping Pam could not hear them, and his lean face darkened ominously.

'Why not?' he demanded, apparently uncaring of their surroundings, and she cast an imploring glance up at him.

'Because I can't,' she whispered, her eyes darting in Adam's direction. 'Please, Dan, don't do this. You're making a scene.'

'This is nothing to what I can do, believe me,' he grated, and she didn't doubt it.

'I can't leave Adam,' she insisted in a low tone. 'Try and understand my position.'

'Why should I? Do you try and understand mine?'

'Dan ...'

'That's my name!'

'Dan, we had all this out before——'

'You wanted to meet my family. Well, you have. What else do you want me to do? You came here. You accepted my invitation——'

'*Your* invitation?'

'What else?'

He was looking down at her as he spoke, and in the fading light she could sense the intensity of his gaze. She could drown in those eyes, she thought, weakening under the physical onslaught of his attraction, and she had to force herself to concentrate on the liquid in her glass as she spoke.

'Your—your aunt implied that she had—offered the invitation,' she said through taut lips, and chanced a glimpse at his expression.

'She did,' he responded, bringing a furrow to her forehead until he elaborated. 'But I asked her to do it.' He paused. 'Will you dance with me now?'

'Dan, she doesn't like me. She doesn't want me here——'

'I do,' he said, and what she saw in his face robbed her of all resistance.

She managed to replace her glass on a passing tray as he drew her after him on to the tiled floor of the patio. She didn't dare to wonder what Adam must be thinking, and presently Dan's arms around her banished all other considerations. She was close against him, her face pressed against the smooth silk of his shirt, his arms encircling her waist so that she was obliged to loop hers around his neck.

'Mmm, I've wanted this,' he muttered, bending his head to nuzzle her ear, and she had to steel herself from resting against him.

'I thought—after that day on the wharf——' she began unsteadily, but his finger across her lips silenced her.

'You didn't think you'd get rid of me that easily, did you?' he mocked gently, and she turned her lips away from the sensual temptation of his.

'How—how did you persuade your aunt to invite me?' she persisted, trying to maintain a detachment she was far from feeling, and he moved his shoulders in a lazy shrug.

'She's not so bad,' he remarked dismissingly, allowing his hand to move from her waist to the silky skin that covered her shoulder blades. 'I like your dress,' he added huskily, 'but I like you better without it....'

'Dan!'

Her protest was almost desperate, and for a few moments they turned in silence round the tiny dance floor. It was hardly dancing, and the music didn't help the way she was feeling. It was a haunting melody, all piano and rhythm guitar, and sung by a sexy young singer whose music was full of mood and innuendo. It seduced the mind as well as the senses, and Julie could feel her emotions responding to its insidious appeal. It wasn't fair, she thought frustratedly, but when Dan's fingers probed inside the low back of her dress she didn't try to stop him. On the contrary, she withdrew her arms from around his neck and slipped them about his waist, inside his jacket, close against the fine silk of his shirt. It brought her closer to him, she could feel the warmth of his body through the thin material, and once again she felt the stirring urgency between his thighs.

When the music finally came to an end, Julie felt almost drugged with emotion, and Dan made no attempt to let her go. 'Come on,' he said, resting his forehead against hers, 'I want to show you something.'

Julie looked up at him helplesly. She was aware that the longer they stood there, the more attention they were drawing to themselves, and while the alternative Dan was offering was dangerous, it was also irresistible in her present condition. With a little sound of protest she acquiesced, nodding her head, and Dan released her only so far as the encircling possession of his arm would allow as he walked her towards the house.

Several people saw them go, but no one Julie recognised, and she silenced her conscience with the unconvincing assurance that she was doing nothing wrong. She had wanted to see Dan's home, or at least the place where he was staying, and now she was being given the chance. Even so, nothing she had seen so far had prepared her for the luxury of the Leytons' house and her eyes widened in stunned disbelief as they entered the massive hall-cum-living room.

She supposed it could be called a cabin. The walls were of wood, certainly, but there the resemblance to a hunter's shelter ended. Forest Bay was a tasteful country residence, a millionaire's retreat, that combined all the comfort of a luxury apartment with the plain fabric of simple elegance. There was lots of leather, squashy leather sofas and chairs, and leather-topped tables that supported a variety of Indian relics. The walls were hung with Indian paintings, and over the massive open fireplace, which could surely roast an ox, were a pair of crossed rifles. But overriding everything was the atmosphere of wealth and affluence, evidenced in the fine silk of the lampshades, the lush velour of the curtains, the glittering crystal that ornamented a polished cabinet, and the rich skin rugs upon the floor.

'Uncle Max collects these things,' Dan remarked, indicating the rifles with a wry grimace. 'Sometimes I think it's a sign of repressed masculinity. Aunt Anthea likes her own way.'

'I can imagine,' agreed Julie with fervour, and Dan's arm tightened protectively.

'You don't have to worry about her,' he asserted huskily, turning his mouth against her cheek, and she felt a shiver of anticipation slide along her spine.

'Is there something you want, Mr Prescott?'

A woman in the uniform of a housekeeper was approaching them across the hall, and Dan shook his head. 'That's okay, Mrs Carling,' he assured her politely. 'I'm just showing Miss Osbourne the house.'

'Yes, sir.'

The woman gave Julie an appraising stare before withdrawing again, however, and Julie began to feel uneasy. The compelling spell the music had cast over her was fading, and common sense began to erode her confidence. 'I—what is it you have to show me?' she asked, linking her fingers together. 'Adam—Adam will be wondering where I am. Perhaps it's not such a good idea, after all. I mean, what will everyone think?'

'The worst, I guess,' Dan admitted laconically, but he did not seem perturbed. 'Relax. Enjoy yourself. That's what you're here for.'

Julie sighed. 'Dan——'

'It's upstairs,' he said. 'What I want to show you.' He released her shoulders to take her hand, drawing her resistingly towards the staircase. 'Will you come with me?'

Julie hung back. 'What is it? What do I have to see? Dan, if this is some trick——'

'It's not.' Though his mouth had hardened slightly. 'Julie, trust me.'

'Can I?'

'Well, can't you?'

Her doubts faltered. 'I suppose so.'

'You know so,' he declared harshly, drawing her towards him. Then, when her lips parted in protest, he added: 'Come on. It won't take long.'

The staircase comprised two flights of stairs that led up to an encircling balcony. Julie reached the top and leaned on the rail overlooking the hall below, and Dan rested his back beside her and folded his arms.

'Out of breath?' he enquired, the blue-grey eyes slightly mocking, and she straightened to gaze at him.

'Are you taking me to your room?' she asked, steeling herself for his reply, but his mouth only curved in lazy humour.

'Miss Osbourne! You surely don't intend some mischief to my body, do you?' he demanded, in a broad Southern accent, and she gave a helpless shrug of her shoulders.

'Dan, please——'

'Follow me,' he interrupted her shortly, and with a feeling of inadequacy, she did so.

A long corridor opened out before them, carpeted in shades of green and gold, with double-panelled doors along its length that were presently closed against them. Wall-lights were set in sconces between the doors, and the silence was barely disturbed by the drifting sounds from the garden. They were alone, and she was completely at his mercy, she thought uneasily, realising that neither David nor Adam knew where she was.

She was about to make some excuse for not going any further when she realised they had reached the end of the corridor. A single door confronted them, set into the wood-work, and totally unlike any of the panelled doors they had passed. A latch secured it in place, and as Julie reached him Dan lifted the latch and the door swung open to reveal a narrow twisting flight of stairs.

Her anxious frown aroused his sympathy, and with a slight smile he said: 'It's not Bluebeard's den, or Rapunzel's tower. Just a room that I want you to see.'

Julie hesitated, and with a sigh Dan went first through the door. After a moment she followed him, curiosity get-ting the better of her, and they climbed the spiral staircase to the tiny turret room above.

It was still light enough to see that the room was furnished as a den, with specially curved bookcases along its circular walls, and a small desk strewn with an assortment of charts and papers. Dan turned on a small lamp, how-ever, and its mellow light showed the ravages that time had wrought. Now Julie was able to see why there was such a musty smell about the place. The books were old and de-caying, and the papers on the desk were sere and yellow with age.

'My grandfather's hideaway,' remarked Dan, watching her reactions. 'He used to come up here to escape my grand-mother, I suspect. She was a woman much like Aunt Anthea'.

Julie shook her head. 'It's a—fantastic place.' She moved to the windows. 'And look at the view!'

'I know.' He came to stand behind her, and although he didn't touch her, she was aware of him with every shred of her being. 'That's what I really wanted to show you. Look here . . .'

He indicated an old-fashioned telescope set on a stand near the windows. It was trained on the sweep of bay beyond the promontory, and although it was almost dark, it was possible to see the lights glinting among the trees at the far side of the water.

Julie adjusted it to her eyes, and then made an unexpected discovery. 'I say,' she exclaimed incredulously, 'that's the hotel, isn't it? Look, Dan, those lights shining over there. It's the hotel, isn't it? Heavens, if it was light——'

'—you could see a lot more,' he finished dryly, bending to look over her shoulder. 'Like the cove below, for instance.'

Julie gasped and turned so quickly she almost knocked him off balance. 'You—you mean, you saw me!' she exclaimed.

Dan straightened, regarding her penitently. 'I'm afraid so,' he admitted, although he didn't sound remorseful.

'You—you trained that telescope on me!'

'Are you shocked?'

Julie could hardly speak. 'But—but I could have been doing anything,' she objected.

'Like swimming in the raw?' He gave a crooked grimace.

'You mean—you came to find me?'

'Hmm—mmm.'

'Oh, Dan!'

'I'd tried for days,' he said wryly. 'That coastline has dozens of inlets, and at first it didn't occur to me that you might be staying at the hotel. I didn't even know there was an hotel until Drew told me.'

Julie bent her head. 'I—I must have been a disappointment.'

'What do you want me to say to that?' he asked huskily. 'Julie, don't make this any harder for me than it already is. You know how I felt when I saw you—how I feel about you still.'

Julie caught her breath. 'We'd better go ...'

'Do you want to?'

She looked up. 'Do you?'

He shook his head, and with a little gulp she turned aside from him to stare unseeingly through the window. In this small room, it was incredibly difficult to remember her earlier intentions. And discovering that their meeting had been no accident filled her with a reluctant excitement. Imagining Dan standing up here, training his telescope on her small cove, was a tantalising experience, and the sigh she uttered revealed the conflicting uncertainty of her emotions.

'Julie,' he said, and she did not resist when his hands drew her back against him. 'Julie, you're tearing me to pieces!'

'I—I think you're doing the same to me,' she confessed, resting her head against him, and with a groan he sought the worn old easy chair behind him, dropping down on to its scarred leather seat and pulling her down on top of him.

His mouth found hers with unerring accuracy, and she was too startled to object. Warm and insistent and subtly compelling, it robbed her of all resistance, and with his hand cupping her neck and his thumb probing the hollows of her ear, she had no will to avoid the hungry pressure of his lips. Her mouth opened under his like a flower to the sun, submitting eagerly to his searching caress, and her hands slipped around his neck, and tangled in the thick smooth hair at his nape. She was gripped with a mindless ecstasy, submerged in a wine-dark sea of emotion that left no room for doubts, but set her heart pounding at a suffocating pace. His mouth caressed her ears and her cheeks, descending with purposeful sensuality to her neck and shoulder, pushing the strap aside and teasing the sensitised skin.

'You don't know what it's been like, staying away from you,' he muttered, threading his fingers through her hair and drawing it across his lips. 'Waiting for Anthea to issue her invitation—dreading the possibility that you might

refuse . . .' His mouth sought hers once again. 'When Brad
told me where you were yesterday, I wanted to kill you!'

Julie drew an unsteady breath, but she couldn't think
coherently at this moment. 'He—he said you had told him
to tell me you—you would see me again,' she whispered.
'I was—afraid.'

'Of me?' he groaned, cupping her face in his hands and
gazing down at her, but she managed to shake her head.

'Of—of myself,' she confessed helplessly. 'Oh, Dan, I
can't think straight when I'm with you.'

His humour was rueful. 'I know the feeling,' he conceded dryly. 'I'm not usually so intense, believe me.'

'I—I expect you usually get what you want more easily,
don't you?' she probed huskily, and his lips twisted in reluctant admission.

'If you mean what I think you mean then I don't think I
should answer that question,' he teased, allowing one tor-
menting finger to trail pleasurably from her chin to the
hidden hollow between her breasts. 'But if it's any con-
solation to you,' he added, his voice deepening as his own
emotions were aroused, 'I've never been this way with any
girl before.'

'No?'

'No.' His eyes were narrowed and disturbingly passionate. 'I don't know what you do to me, but I don't seem able
to think of anything else.'

'Oh, Dan . . .' For the first time, she drew his head to
hers, and her lips played with his. 'You do things to me,
too.'

'What things?' he demanded, imprisoning her mouth
beneath his, as her fingers sought the buttons of his shirt,
and she pressed herself closer.

'I like looking at you,' she confessed, drawing back to
stroke his chest with her palms. 'You're very—brown,
aren't you? Very brown——'

'Dear God, Julie, what do you think I'm made of?' he

groaned, dragging her hands away from him, and as he did so someone called his name. The sound was insistent, a feminine sound, that echoed hollowly up the spiral stairs. Julie barely had time to struggle off Dan's knees before footsteps accompanied a repetition of the summons. Dan tried to stop her, but she wouldn't let him even though he made no attempt to get up. He just sat there, looking soberly up at her, one leg draped insolently over the arm of the chair, and she wished desperately that she had the right to be here with him.

The girl who erupted into the tiny turret room dazzled Julie. Tall and slim and willowy, with Afro-curled hair tinted a startling shade of red, she was wearing a scarlet jump-suit that somehow just failed from clashing madly. The jump-suit was made of satin, and clung to every line of her slender body, and it was obvious even to the least perceptive of eyes that she wore nothing beneath it. Blue eyes surveyed them from beneath artificially-long lashes, and black mascara had been used to elongate them to good effect. Combined with shiny red lip-gloss, her make-up was perfect, and Julie wondered who on earth she could be.

'Darling,' the girl exclaimed, as soon as she saw Dan. 'There you are! I've been looking everywhere for you.' Her eyes flickered scathingly over Julie before she continued: 'Mommy's simply livid, darling. You've been neglecting your duties. You know how she depends on you to keep all the little ladies occupied.'

'Go away, Corinne, there's a good girl.' Dan's words were mild, but no one could doubt the menace behind them. 'Tell your mother I'm busy.'

Corinne Leyton, for Julie could only assume that this was Dan's cousin, made a sound of frustration. 'Don't be a meanie, Dan,' she protested, approaching his chair and stroking his sleeve with scarlet-tipped fingernails. 'Darling, you know what Mommy's like,' she added wheedlingly, finger-walking her way up to his neck. 'If she doesn't get her own way, she'll blame me, and I might have to tell her where you are and who you're with . . .'

Julie was feeling a little sick now. The recklessness of her own behaviour was hard enough to justify without being made to watch Dan being mauled by this female predator. It was obvious from Corinne's attitude that she considered she had some prior claim to his attentions, and judging from the way she was leaning over him, she did not consider Julie any competition.

'If you'll excuse me——' she began, only to halt uncertainly as Dan sprang up from the chair, brushing his cousin aside and grasping her arm with possessive fingers.

'You don't have to go,' he muttered, his eyes still smouldering with emotion, and for a moment Julie wavered.

But then the recollection of where she was and how she had got here came to sober her. 'Oh—yes, I do,' she got out unsteadily. 'Adam—Adam will be looking for me——'

'To hell with Adam!' he snapped, apparently indifferent to Corinne's shocked disapproval. 'I want you, Julie, no one else!'

'Dan!' It was Corinne who interposed herself between them then, pressing her fist against his shoulder. 'Don't be a fool!'

'Get out of my way, Corinne!'

There was no mistaking his accent now. It was not his polite English heritage that faced his cousin with ice-cold aggression, and Julie felt her hold on reality slipping. This couldn't really be happening to her, she thought disbelievingly. It was some awful dream she was having and very soon she would wake up to the warm security that Adam represented. Dan did not offer security. He only offered himself, the disturbingly sensual man he was, and that only on a part-time basis.

With a twist of her wrist she broke free of him, and he was baulked by Corinne's clinging fingers as he tried to go after her. Julie's heels clattered noisily on the stairs, as

Corinne's had done on the way up, but soon enough she had reached the long strip of carpet that led to safety and sanity, and she walked swiftly along it.

'Julie!' She heard his voice behind her, but she didn't turn, although his quicker stride easily brought him abreast of her. 'Julie, for heaven's sake,' he muttered savagely, 'stop and listen to what I have to say!'

'No.' She shook her head and continued to shake it as she reached the head of the stairs, pressing her palms to her ears to silence his bitter protests. 'Don't say anything else, Dan, please. I don't want to hear it. I don't want to listen to you——'

'Julie!'

The torment in his voice was almost her undoing. Her head jerked helplessly in his direction, and she was torn by the anguish in his face, but she couldn't stop now. Somehow she had to destroy the feelings he aroused inside her, and so long as she was with him that was impossible to do.

She was partway down the second flight when she realised he had stopped at the halfway landing, and blinking she saw the reason why. As she self-consciously removed her hands from her ears, she saw the hall below was now milling with people, all sheltering from the sudden shower of rain that had driven them indoors. And watching her descent with varying degrees of hostility were Pam, David, Adam—and Anthea Leyton.

CHAPTER SIX

THE remainder of the evening was a disaster. How could it have been anything else? Julie tormented herself later that night, lying sleepless in her cabin. The worst that could happen had happened, and the emptiness of her future stretched ahead of her in cold isolation.

She didn't know which had hurt most—suffering the censuring silence of her friends, or having to watch Dan making himself amenable to his aunt's other guests. It had been bad enough knowing her behaviour had been unforgivable without being made forcibly aware that Dan appeared to have recovered himself remarkably quickly. Observing his easy conquest of men and women alike, watching that quizzical smile come and go, she had been torn by the growing conviction that he had been lying to her all along, that he had not been as distracted as he had pretended, and when he took his cousin on to the dance floor, Julie had turned so that she could not even see him.

Of course, that had been after the icy reception that had greeted her return. She had wanted to apologise, to try and explain to Adam that what had happened would never happen again, but neither he nor David appeared to be speaking to her, and it was left to Pam to suggest they might visit the powder room.

Once there, Julie had realised why the two men had looked at her so contemptuously. She had Dan's mark all over her, from the tumbled curtain of her silky hair to the shiny bareness of her mouth. She could imagine what they had thought of her, what everyone here must be thinking of her, and she had cringed at the thought of returning to the party. Did they imagine she and Dan had been to bed together? They had had the time, goodness knows, and her flesh crawled at the humiliation he had wrought.

'Couldn't you at least have repaired your make-up?' Pam exclaimed, speaking for the first time since she had suggested they leave the two men, and Julie sank down weakly on to the padded stool before the vanity mirror. Fortunately the powder room was almost empty, and the two other occupants were more interested in their own conversation than in Julie's ravaged features.

'No,' she said now, moving her shoulders helplessly. 'Pam, I——'

'Don't try to explain yourself to me,' the older girl interposed swiftly. 'Really, Julie, I wish you wouldn't. This whole outing has turned into a fiasco, and I wish I hadn't come.'

'You wish!' Julie reached for a tissue and began massaging the skin around her nose and mouth. 'Pam, might I remand you, *you* wanted to come!'

Pam sighed, and as if giving in, she sank down on to the stool beside her. 'All right,' she said. 'So I'm to blame. But, for heaven's sake, why did you go off with him?'

Julie bent her head. 'You wouldn't understand.'

'Try me.'

Julie sighed. 'What if I told you I loved him? What then?'

'Julie!' Pam was aghast.

'I know. Crazy, isn't it?' Julie indicated Pam's evening bag. 'Do you have any powder base or lipstick? I didn't think to bring anything with me.'

Pam rummaged in her bag and brought out a comb, a compact and a lipstick. Then, while Julie endeavoured to keep her hand steady enough to apply the make-up, she said desperately: 'I never expected this to happen, Julie, believe me! Oh, I know what I said about dating Dan Prescott, but I never intended you to take him seriously. I—I just wanted you to see that there were other men in the world besides Adam.'

Julie shrugged. 'Well, you certainly succeeded.' She paused to give her friend a half sympathetic glance. 'Don't worry, Pam, I'm not blaming you. It's all my own fault, and I should have known better. I will in future.'

Pam bit her lip. 'Did—did anything happen? I mean, you looked so—so——'

'Dishevelled?' suggested Julie tautly, but Pam shook her head.'

'No. No—dazed! Julie, did he——'

'No.' Julie's tone was flat now. 'He hasn't seduced me, if that's what you're thinking.'

'Thank God for that!' Pam was fervent. 'Oh, Julie, I thought David was going to blow his top when Anthea Leyton asked where you were.'

Julie frowned. 'She asked where I was?'

'Yes. About fifteen minutes ago.' She shivered. 'Oh, Julie, I don't like that woman. She's horrible!'

'Why? What did she say?'

'Well, at first she was very polite.' Pam paused to replace her compact in her bag. 'She asked if we were enjoying our-selves, you know the sort of thing—isn't it a warm evening —have you had some champagne—so pleased you could come, etc. Then she asked where you were. I had to tell her the last time I'd seen you, you'd been dancing with her nephew, and her whole manner changed, just like that.' She snapped her fingers, and then looked away in embarrass-ment as she realised she had attracted the attention of the women at the other end of the room.

'Was she rude?' Julie applied the lipstick with trembling fingers.

'She was—insulting. She said she hoped you were not going to make a nuisance of yourself, that Dan spent his time extricating himself from relationships with girls who persisted in imagining he was seriously interested in them.

She laughed—you know, one of those supercilious sophisticated laughs, saying that it was just as well her stepdaughter had a sense of humour, otherwise she might choose to give Dan a taste of his own medicine.'

Julie tasted the sourness of bile in the back of her throat. 'Her—stepdaughter?' she echoed faintly. '*Corinne* Leyton?'

'That's right. Have you seen her? She's wearing a jumpsuit that's practically indecent——'

'I've seen her,' Julie put in flatly, and Pam nodded in sympathy.

'Anyway,' she went on, apparently unaware that Julie was paler now than she had been before, 'David got really mad. He said he didn't know about any of the other girls Dan's supposed to have dated, but that he—*Dan*—was making all the running so far as you were concerned. Of course, that didn't suit her, and Adam finished it off by saying that you and he were going to be married in the fall.'

'Oh, Pam!'

Julie closed her eyes in agony, and with reluctance Pam concluded what she had to say. 'She had to accept it,' she said doggedly. 'What else could she do? Then, ten minutes later, you came down the stairs as if he'd been all over you, and I guess we all felt pretty foolish!'

'Oh, God!' It was worse than she had imagined, and all she wanted was to run and hide, somewhere, anywhere, away from here, where she could lick her wounds in private.

But she had had to go back to the party, and the only way she could do that was by adopting an air of indifference she found almost impossible to sustain. Nevertheless, it enabled her to meet the eyes of Anthea Leyton and her friends without flinching, and if she wavered a little every time Dan looked in her direction, that was easily remedied by avoiding him altogether. Certainly, he made no further attempt to come near him, and she guessed his aunt's warning had been sufficient to deter him.

It was harder coping with Adam and David. David was brusque and abrupt, speakingly only when obliged to do so, but over the plates of steak and salad that were served by the uniformed staff, Adam unbent sufficiently to ask whether she was all right.

'Of course. Why shouldn't I be?' she had countered stiffly, unable to relax even with him in case her whole façade of composure should collapse; and he had shrugged his slim shoulders in confusion, obviously bewildered by this unexpected turn of events.

They were all relieved when they could reasonably make their escape. Maxwell Leyton wished them farewell, without the inimical presence of his wife, and Julie climbed into the launch eagerly, desperate to put some distance between herself and the man standing watching them from the top of the steps. He must have heard them saying their goodbyes, she thought bitterly, and turned her head as a shadowy figure blended itself with him, a slender wraith outlined in scarlet.

At the hotel, when she might have spoken to Adam, he took himself off to his cabin with only the briefest of goodnights, and left with Pam and David, Julie could only offer her apologies.

'Forget it,' David advised brusquely, his expression more sympathetic than it had been earlier. 'I warned you about Dan Prescott. Perhaps now you'll believe me when I say he's bad news!'

'Yes, David.'

Julie conceded the point and wished them goodnight, but she knew it wasn't going to be that easy to put Dan out of her thoughts, in spite of his duplicity.

In the morning she awakened with a muzzy head, due no doubt to the amount of champagne she had consumed the night before. She was not used to such high living, but she had used the wine to dull the sharp edge of vulnerability. Now, she wished she could do the same again, and exist in a numb, unfeeling state until the rawness of her emotions began to heal. Perhaps after she got back to England, she thought, clutching blindly for a lifeline, and then realised she might well have forfeited that security once and for all.

She was drinking coffee at her table in the dining room, both hands cupped protectively round the cup, when Adam joined her. He slipped into the seat opposite with the least amount of fuss, and then looked at her with wary eyes. Julie returned his stare rather nervously, her smile only tentative, but Adam broke the ice by leaning towards her and saying:

'I thought you might not want to talk to me—after last night. I let you down, I know, going to bed like that, but I needed to think. Now I have to know where I stand.'

Julie put down her cup with careful precision, then clasped her fingers together. 'Where you stand?' she said, echoing his words. 'Where do you stand, Adam? Am I beyond absolution?'

'No!' Adam's response was sure and firm. 'At least, not if you don't want to be. Look, Julie, I realised something was wrong on the way up here—I told you that. Why couldn't you have been honest with me then?'

Julie shrugged. 'There was nothing—there *is* nothing—to be honest about.'

'But you can't deny that you went off with Prescott last evening, that you—well, had some—contact with him.'

Julie bent her head. 'No, I can't deny that.'

'So tell me about it. Tell me what he means to you.'

That was more difficult. Julie looked up. 'You won't like it.'

'I don't particularly like any of this, Julie.'

She sighed. 'I'm attracted to him.'

'Are you in love with him?'

'Perhaps.'

'I see.' Adam did not sound entirely surprised. 'And what about him? How does he feel?'

'It's not the same.' Julie could be certain of that. 'You heard what his aunt said—Pam told me. I think she outlined the situation pretty well.'

'Yes.' Adam was thoughtful. 'It's not a relationship the Prescotts would welcome.'

'Do you think I don't know that?' Julie clenched her fists.

'So how far has this relationship gone?'

'I haven't slept with him, if that's what you're suggesting.'

'I'm relieved.' He made a dismissing gesture. 'It's better if these things can be kept simple.'

Simple! Julie's heart contracted. If only it was simple!

'And what about us?' Adam asked now. 'You know how I feel about you, how I have always felt. Our relationship—well, it's always meant more to me than anything else, and —and I think your father knew that and depended on it.'

'Oh, Adam . . .'

'Let's get something straight, shall we?' He reached across and covered one of her hands with his. 'So far, I've made no demands upon you. Ever since I came to fetch you home from St Helena's, I have considered you—respected you—endeavoured to give you time to regain your balance.'

'I know that, Adam.'

'But that's not to say, I don't love you, or desire you, just as much as any younger man. I know I'm seventeen years older than you are, I know that must seem a terrible gap to someone of your age——'

'No, Adam!'

'—but I've always considered you a mature and capable young woman, perfectly able to share my life, my work, and my love. To be the only woman in my life, the hostess in my house, the mistress of my fate—this is what I'm offering you, and it's still yours, if you choose to take it.'

'Adam ... Adam ...' She turned her hand so that she could squeeze his. 'I know how kind you've been, I know I couldn't have managed these past weeks without you, even here, knowing you were always there, always waiting, caring ...' She sighed. 'I don't think I have changed. I think this—this affair with—with—well, you know—it hasn't altered my opinion of you, it's—it's strengthened it. I don't want to change anything. We—we are still the same people, aren't we?'

'Of course we are.' Adam's doubts had cleared away, and his smile was confident. 'Oh, Julie, I'm so relieved. You don't know what a terrible night I spent!'

'I do.' Julie's smile was tremulous. 'Mine wasn't too great either.'

Adam nodded. 'You know what I think? I think we should get away from here, right away. And I don't just mean Toronto. Let's pack our bags and leave altogether. We could go to the coast. California! Spend a couple of months travelling. I need a break, too. We might even get married before going home.'

Julie couldn't prevent the sudden surge of despondency that gripped her at his words. It was what she had wanted to hear, she told herself fiercely, of course it was! So why did her spirits abruptly sink so low, and misery envelop her at the thought of leaving this place?

'What do you say?'

Adam was waiting for her answer, and she knew she had to make a decision. Who was she fooling, after all? There was nothing for her here. Nothing but pain and unhappiness and humiliation.

'If—if that's what you want, Adam,' she answered, picking up her coffee cup again, hiding her uncertainty behind its sheltering thickness. 'You know I wanted to leave days ago.'

'Good. That's settled, then. We'll leave this afternoon.'

Get the exciting love-filled romances *you* want to read...
CHOOSE ONE OF THESE OFFERS NOW!

4 Free Harlequin Presents!

Take these 4 FREE Harlequin Presents novels ... they are our gift to you just to introduce you to the convenience of Harlequin Reader Service, the fastest, surest way we know for you to receive the novels you love to read. As a member, you pay nothing extra for the convenience of receiving your novels by mail, no postage, no handling, no extra charges!

Your free gift includes:
Gates of Steel
by Anne Hampson
Helen entered into a loveless marriage in a mountain village in Cyprus, never dreaming she would someday find herself in a physical and emotional turmoil.

No Quarter Asked
by Janet Dailey
Stacey chose a deserted cabin in Texas to start her life over again, but she soon discovered she was an unwelcome visitor.

Sweet Revenge
by Anne Mather
He had looks, money and a castle in Portugal, but could he hold on to this elusive, strong-willed woman he craved?

Devil in a Silver Room
by Violet Winspear
Fate had brought Margo to the remote French Chateau, and now the ruthless brother of the man she had once loved, desired her.

OR choose this FREE Harlequin Catalog!

This is the catalog that lists many Harlequin novels still available to you right now. This is one handy comprehensive list for you to keep absolutely FREE — with no obligation whatsoever. If you wish, you may order from the catalog at any time. Choose the books you want to read, when you want to read them.

Send for your 4 FREE *Harlequin Presents* novels or your FREE Harlequin Catalog today

Mail the attached postage paid reply card today! ▶

Choose the offer that best suits your needs!

☑ Check the appropriate box.

'*This afternoon!*' Her cup clattered into its saucer again at that.

'Why not? I'm sure your friend Galloway won't object to driving us to the airport. And first class seats are usually available.' He consulted his watch, and then went on: 'I happen to know there's a flight from Toronto to Vancouver at eight. That gives us plenty of time.'

Julie was in a state of shock. She had expected Adam to make arrangements for them to leave tomorrow, or even the next day, but today!

'Don't you think that's rather—rushing things?' she ventured. 'And it's very short notice for Pam.'

Adam looked at her squarely. 'A clean break, that's what I always recommend,' he declared. 'A clean break, and a fresh start. We can always invite the Galloways to stay with us in England after we're home. You know your friends will always be welcome.'

Julie couldn't take it all in. Half of her was applauding his single-minded strength of purpose, but the other half of her was holding back, protesting at the impulsiveness of his action, clinging to the present with clenched fists.

'Not today,' she said at last, unable to meet him all the way. 'Adam, I need time—time to pack, time to say good-bye to people. To say goodbye to Brad! We've been such good friends. I can't just run out on him.'

'Oh, very well.' Adam gave in with good grace, aware that he had won a minor victory nonetheless. 'Tomorrow, then. Tomorrow afternoon. I promise you, you won't regret it. I'll make you happy, Julie. It's all I ever wanted to do.'

Julie smiled, but it was a fleeting illumination, and when the waitress returned to take Adam's order, she excused herself to go and start packing.

'I'll come to your cabin after breakfast,' Adam called as she reached the door into the hall, and she nodded a little absently as she went out.

Crossing the tree-shaded square to her cabin, however,

she was struck again by pangs of homesickness. It was
curious, but this place had come to mean home to her, and
England and the house in Hampstead, seemed a long way
away. She had to leave sooner or later, she told herself
fiercely, but the suddenness of Adam's decision had left her
cold and strangely bereft.

Her cabin seemed shadowy after the brilliant sunshine
outside, and as usual it took her eyes a few moments to
adjust. Closing the door, she leant back against it wearily,
allowing her lids to droop against the prospect ahead of
her. In a minute she would have to start clearing her
things from the cabin, and all the little mementoes she had
collected would all have to be stowed in her suitcases. It
was not a task she looked forward to, particularly as she
instinctively knew that Adam would not want them clutter-
ing up any room he had to live in.

'Hello, Julie!'

The low, distinctive masculine voice was shatteringly
familiar, and her eyes opened wide, darting disbelievingly
across the room. It was too early in the morning to be
hallucinating, she thought, but the man propped negligently
against the end of her bed had to be a figment of her over-
active imagination, and she blinked rapidly in the hope that
he might disappear. But he didn't. He straightened from his
position and came towards her, and sheer unadulterated
panic gripped her.

Her fingers groped desperately behind her, searching for
the handle, but she couldn't find it, and before she could
turn Dan had imprisoned her where she was, his hands
resting against the door at either side of her.

'Oh, Julie,' he said, and there was a driven note in his
voice now. 'What am I going to do about you?'

'How—how did you get here?' she stammered, avoiding
his eyes, concentrating on the column of his throat rising
from the unbuttoned neckline of his shirt.

'Brad told me which was your cabin,' he conceded flatly.

'Don't blame him—I bribed him to tell me. I can be unscrupulous if I have to.'

'Don't I know it?' she got out unsteadily, pressing her palms against the cool wood at her sides. 'Did—did you and—and Corinne enjoy yourselves after I left?'

He didn't answer her, and her eyes darted upward to find him watching her with weary resignation. 'Do you expect me to answer that?' he asked. 'What do you think we did? Go to bed together?'

'It—it wouldn't be unreasonable in the circumstances, would it?' she demanded jerkily, and he expelled his breath on a long sigh.

'What circumstances?'

'You and she. Your aunt told Pam and David and——'

'I don't care what the hell my aunt told anyone,' he cut in savagely. 'Corinne and I mean nothing to one another. We never have. And if you think it's on offer, then you'll have to take my word that I've never sampled the merchandise.'

'Then why did your aunt——'

'Why do you think?' he snapped, his temper giving way. 'She knows the way I feel about you—she's not stupid. She's just using every weapon in her power to drive you away.'

'And she's succeeded,' declared Julie tremulously. 'I—we —Adam and I are leaving tomorrow.'

'Leaving?'

'For California. He wants us to have a holiday together before we go home to England—to the house my father left me.'

'William Osbourne,' muttered Dan broodingly. 'Yes, I know.' Then he shook his head. 'But you can't leave, Julie. I won't let you.'

'How are you going to stop me? I'm going to marry Adam.'

'Are you?' With a lithe movement he closed the space

between them, crushing her back against the door with the weight of his body. 'And does he know how you feel about me?'

'As—as a matter of fact, he does,' Julie got out breathlessly, finding it difficult to draw any air into her lungs. 'Dan, take your hands off me! I'm not your possession. Just because——'

'What did you tell him?' he demanded harshly. 'Did you explain how we met? I can imagine he would find that very amusing. And what did you say in your own defence? That I chased you, that I forced you to do things you wouldn't otherwise have thought of?'

'No! No!' Julie jerked her head back. 'I—I just told him I—I was attracted to you——'

'Attracted to me?' Dan shook his head. 'Well, okay. That's one way of putting it, I guess. And he'll marry you, knowing that?'

'Of course.'

'*Oh, God!*'

'Dan, Adam's not like you——'

'That's the truth. He's not,' he conceded harshly, his hands at her waist tightening painfully. 'Julie,' he bent his head towards her, and she was disturbingly aware of the parted invitation of his mouth. 'Julie, don't do this to me— *to us*! We're so good together!'

'And is that all you think matters?' she got out unsteadily. 'Be-being good together? There—there's more to life than—than——'

'Sex,' he interposed smoothly. 'Why don't you say it? Or is that word not part of your vocabulary?'

Julie pursed her lips, pressing her fists against his chest. 'Just let me go, Dan,' she pleaded. 'Adam will be here soon. He—he's just having his breakfast, then he's coming to help me pack.'

'To leave.'

'Yes.'

Dan's lips curled. 'Well now, why don't I just hang around until he comes? Perhaps I can give him some pointers about you——'

'You wouldn't!'

Julie's words were torn from her, her head tipped back in dismay, eyes wide with consternation. She had never looked more desirable, and Dan's expression softened slightly.

'Kiss me, Julie,' he said roughly. 'Just one more time. Then I'll go, I promise.'

'You—you promise?' she whispered, not altogether convinced of his sincerity, and he nodded.

'Scouts honour,' he agreed mockingly, and cupped his hand possessively around her throat.

She had hoped to keep it brief, but when she reached up to touch his lips and his mouth parted over hers, she knew that was not his intention. Her breathing seemed suspended as he moved his head from side to side against the resisting barrier of her lips, arousing a response she had to fight to overcome. He did not force her, and although her fists were still balled against him, they offered little opposition as he continued to hold her.

'Coward,' he said at last, his voice muffled against her cheek, and soon as she opened her mouth to protest, she knew she had lost. Her senses were already swimming, and when his lips touched hers, she had no more strength to combat her own desires. Weakness overwhelmed her, and her hands uncurled to spread against his shoulders.

When Dan finally lifted his head, his face was pale beneath his tan, but he stepped back from her abruptly and pushed both hands through the virile thickness of his hair. 'Okay,' he said, as she endeavoured to gather her scattered senses, pulling the lapels of her denim jacket together, checking the zip of her jeans, anything to avoid the inevitability of their parting. 'Walk me down to the marina.'

'That—that wasn't part of our bargain,' she objected, and then submitted when he turned hurt eyes in her direction. 'All—all right. But I'll have to be quick or Adam will wonder where I am.'

'Right.'

Dan waited until she had straightened and then wrenched open the door, blinking as the brilliant sunlight flooded into the room. He allowed her to precede him, and then closed the door behind them and matched his lean stride to hers as they walked to the head of the steps that led down to the small breakwater David had built.

She saw the yacht Brad had gone into such raptures about as they walked along the jetty. It truly was a magnificent craft, all cold steel and mahogany, its sleek racing lines combined with big-boat luxury. The afterdeck was furnished with cushioned basketweave chairs and tables, and steps led down to the cabins below which Brad had described in enthusiastic detail, while the wheelhouse possessed two squashy leather armchairs for the pilot and a companion.

'So that's the *Spirit of Atlantis*,' Julie observed tautly, needing to say something to break the uneasy silence between them, and Dan inclined his head.

'That's right. D'you want to look around?'

'Oh, no—no,' Julie shook her head vigorously, trying to remain cool, when the knowledge of how he could make her feel was turning like a knife inside her. 'I—it's beautiful, isn't it? No wonder Brad was so impressed.'

'Come aboard,' Dan urged tersely, glancing round at the other vessels rocking on their moorings, and she felt the devastating pull of his attraction.

'I—I can't——'

'Why not?' He bent to untie one of the ropes that kept it steady. Then he straightened and looked into her eyes. 'Julie, don't make me say goodbye to you here on the jetty.'

'Dan, that's not fair,' she protested. 'We said goodbye up there.'

'Did we?' He held her gaze. 'Are you going to deny that you'd like to repeat it?'

'Oh, Dan ...'

'At least step on to the deck,' he suggested, possessing himself of one of her hands. 'Look, it's easy. Just step across the gap——'

'I know how to get on board,' she exclaimed, inhaling indignantly. 'Dan——'

'I'll help you,' he said, ignoring her objections, and before she realised what he was doing, he had picked her up and deposited her on the afterdeck.

'Dan——' she began again, as he bent to release another rope, but he continued to ignore her, and she realised with a mixture of dismay and excitement that the yacht was definitely breaking free of the mooring. 'Dan, this is crazy!'

'I know,' he answered, but his face had recovered a little of its colour. 'However, we can't all live by the book, can we? And I have no intention of letting you spend today with Price.'

CHAPTER SEVEN

JULIE supposed she could have swum ashore if she had wanted to. After all, Dan had to go for'ard to start the two powerful engines, but the jeans and denim jacket she was wearing were a definite deterrent, and she doubted she could strip in the time she had. Instead she stood at the rail, one hand gripping the steel pillar that supported the upper deck, and watched the little harbour receding swiftly behind them.

'Are you mad at me?' her captor demanded softly, his breath fanning her ear, and she turned swiftly to face him.

'What do you think?' she exclaimed, emotion bringing a break to her voice. 'Adam will know where I've gone. Brad is bound to confess when I am missing.'

'So what?' Dan's lean face was sombre. 'You're not Adam Price's possession.'

'I'm not yours either!'

'Is that right?'

'Yes,' she declared fiercely, and he shrugged his broad shoulders.

'Well, we'll see,' he averred flatly, and turned back towards the wheel.

Julie took another anxious look over her shoulder and then sank down weakly on to one of the cushioned loungers. She wasn't really afraid, only apprehensive, but she couldn't help wondering what Dan intended doing with her, and what Adam's reactions might be. He was probably only taking her for a sail, she told herself firmly. It was not as if he was abducting her, and once they got back she would explain to Adam how it had happened. Whether or not he would believe her was not in question. Adam knew she would not lie to him.

With the cool breeze off the lake fanning her cheeks, it was not unpleasant sitting there, and she half wished she could relax and take off her denim jacket. She had put the jacket on over a cotton shirt deliberately because she knew how much Adam deplored bare arms, but now her skin prickled in protest against the coarse fabric. Dan had no such problem. In his usual narrow-fitting jeans and a collarless sweat shirt that exposed every muscle of his hard body he looked cool and controlled, and very much in command of the situation. He was lounging lazily on one of the leather chairs at the wheel, casually studying a map he had spread out on the control panel in front of him.

Now that Julie noticed it, she could see the yacht was very comprehensively equipped with instruments. Various dials and gauges indicated a sophisticated communications system, and most significantly of all, there was a slim radio telephone.

Pressing down on the arms of her chair, she pushed herself to her feet and strolled with assumed indolence towards him. He noted her movements out of the corner of his eye, but he didn't make any move towards her, and she pushed her hands into her jacket pockets to hide their agitation.

'What—what are all these dials?' she asked at last, forced to say something, and he moved his shoulders in an offhand gesture.

'Oil and gas pressures, temperature gauge, echo-sounder, auto-pilot, radar——'

'*Radar!*' She was astounded.

'It's a sophisticated boat,' he remarked expressionlessly, and she nodded helplessly.

'I believe it.'

Unable to resist, she leaned over his shoulder to study the dials more closely, and he turned his head to look at her. He was too close, narrowed eyes focused on her mouth, and she quickly straightened again and ran a nervous finger round the inside of her collar.

'Take it off,' he advised, observing her discomfort. 'And those, too,' he added, indicating her jeans. 'Or you're going to be pretty hot by this afternoon.'

'This afternoon!' Julie was aghast. 'You can't mean to keep me out all afternoon!'

'Why not?' He tipped his head on one side, but there was no humour in his expression. 'Don't you think I'll do it? I can assure you I will.'

'You're mad!'

'Just desperate,' he conceded dryly. 'Now, if you'll give me a few minutes, I'll finish plotting our course——'

'Your course!' she burst out frustratedly, and without really considering the futility of what she was doing, she snatched at the radio telephone.

Of course, he removed it from her resisting fingers without too much effort, and she realised she had probably destroyed her only chance of thwarting him. He would be on his guard now, and she might never get the opportunity again.

'Adam will come looking for me,' she warned, clutching at straws, and Dan gave her a questioning look.

'In what? A helicopter?' he enquired. 'I doubt he'll find us in anything less. He doesn't know these islands. I do.'

'You—you arrogant devil!'

'Relax, why don't you? Go make us a cup of coffee, if you want something to do. Or there's beer and Coke in the freezer, and ice, too, if you want it.'

Julie stared at him resentfully for a few seconds longer, then she turned away. 'You'll make me hate you,' she declared childishly, and he made a sound of indifference.

'That's better than nothing,' he remarked, bending his head to the map once more. 'Oh, and by the way, you'll find a bikini in the locker. I'd put it on, if I were you. It might cool you down.'

She was tempted to defy him, but she was beginning to feel really uncomfortable, and tossing off the jacket with ill-grace, she swung herself down the steps.

The cabin below was just as impressive as the control panel above. Sheathed teak panelling, wall-to-wall carpeting, matching velvet curtains—it was a luxury apartment in miniature, and unable to resist the temptation to explore, Julie ventured forward into the two double cabins, one with an enormous double bunk, and the other with two singles. Each of the cabins had its adjoining shower and toilet compartment, and she discovered a third bathroom next door to the kitchen, with a real bath in it, and not just a shower.

There were fitted cupboards in the cabins, and deciding that Dan's suggestion had given her justification to open them, she looked inside. They were disappointingly empty. Just a pair of canvas shoes had been tossed in the bottom of one tall cubicle, and another produced a rubber wet-suit and some oxygen cylinders.

Shrugging, she went back into the second cabin, and on impulse opened a locker set high on the wall above one of the single bunks. This was more successful. The locker contained a pair of jeans, several thick sweaters, and a pair of men's pyjamas. It encouraged her to look in one on the opposite wall, and here she found what she was really looking for, a cotton shirt—and two bikinis.

The bikinis were much more daring than anything she had ever possessed, and she guessed rather unwillingly that they probably belonged to Corinne. One was yellow, a rather repulsive shade, Julie thought, and she could imagine how it looked with Corinne's red hair. The other was brown and delightfully simple, but she viewed it with some misgivings. Despite the discrepancies in their height, and the fact that Corinne was obviously slimmer, it would probably fit her, but she shrank from the possibility of Corinne's reactions if she ever found out who had been wearing her swimsuit.

Realising that she was wasting time, she carried it into the double-bunked cabin and quickly stripped off her clothes. There was no lock on the door, and she wondered apprehensively what she would do if Dan got suspicious and came looking for her. But he didn't, and she put the bikini on, grimacing at her reflection in the long narrow mirror beside the vanity unit.

As she had expected, it was a perfect fit, and very becoming. More becoming than her own, she acknowledged reluctantly, allowing for the fact that it was a little too brief. It revealed the swell of her hips and the curving length of leg below, and she wondered if she really wanted to display herself like that. With a feeling of resignation, she reached for her jeans and put them on again, over the briefs. The bra would suffice, she decided, remembering that scene by the lake. It would be foolish to affect modesty after the intimacy of their embrace, and without giving herself time to change her mind about that too, she walked quickly through to the living area.

The galley was equally as well equipped as the rest of the craft. As well as the stove and refrigerator, there was a dish-washer and sink-disposal unit, and a variety of gadgets for peeling, dicing and liquidising food. The cupboards were well stocked with tinned and other convenience foods, and Julie paused to wonder who spent time aboard.

She found the coffee without too much difficulty, and a percolator, but after a moment's hesitation she decided not to make a hot drink. It was hot enough already, and instead she extracted a couple of cans of Coke from the fridge, and clutching them against her, she climbed the steps once more.

The yacht was plunging a little as it rode the waves, and she saw with concern that they were well out from the shore now, and in deeper waters that she had hitherto sailed. The cluster of islands she had explored were away to their right while on their left was the mound of the island known as the Giant's Tomb. This was obviously not their destination, however, and her heart flipped a beat as she saw the great expanse of water ahead of them.

'Here's your Coke,' she said, approaching Dan reluctantly and offering him a can, and he took it with a wry smile.

'Coke! How nice,' he acknowledged mockingly, and she realised he would probably have preferred beer. But before she could offer to change it he had opened the can and raised the can to his lips, and she shrugged rather awkwardly as he wiped his mouth on the back of his hand. 'That's cute!' he remarked, waving the can towards her outfit. 'A bra but no briefs! I wonder what happened to them.'

Julie tugged aggravatedly at the ring tab of the can. 'Unlike your cousin, I'm not used to going around half naked,' she declared tightly, and glimpsed his smile before he turned back to his charts. 'Anyway, where are you taking me? Don't I have a right to know?'

'Sure.' He jabbed a finger at the parchment. 'Here. That's where we're going.'

Julie stepped forward warily and took a hasty look at where he was pointing. Then she gasped. 'But—but that's right over there!'

'That's right.' He finished his Coke at a gulp. 'They're the islands that used to be used as lookout points by the Hurons.'

'The Indians?' Julie was impressed in spite of herself.

'You got it.' Dan turned to look at her again. 'So why don't you just stop fighting me and enjoy yourself?'

'I have packing to do——'

'The hell with that!' Dan's mouth thinned. 'You're not leaving, Julie.'

With a feeling of impotence she turned away, unwilling

to argue with him further. What was the point of making him angry? Until she could get off this boat, she was in his hands.

She returned to the afterdeck and after a few restless moments leaning on the rail, watching the places she knew and recognised recede into the distance, she put down her Coke and climbed the ladder to the upper deck. It was more breezy up here, but she found that if she stretched out on the deck itself she was sheltered by the low metal barrier that surrounded it. It was a sun-trap, and she moved sinuously, finding a more comfortable position.

She had been lying there perhaps fifteen minutes when Dan came to find her. She was unaware of his approach until he spoke, and then she jack-knifed into a sitting position, staring at him resentfully.

'Having fun?' he enquired dryly, and she tilted her head aggressively.

'Oughtn't you to be steering this thing?' she demanded, and he shrugged indifferently.

'There's the wheel, if you want to take charge of it,' he remarked, stepping over her legs, and she noticed the secondary steering mechanism. 'But no sweat. It steers itself pretty satisfactorily.'

'You think you're so clever, don't you?' she accused him bitterly, resentful that he had shed his jeans and shirt and was now wearing only navy cotton shorts. The fact that the shorts displayed the muscular length of his legs to good advantage was an additional source of irritation, particularly when he caught her looking at him, and she deliberately turned on to her stomach and buried her face on her folded arms.

It wasn't a happy solution. She couldn't see him, and consequently she didn't know where he was or what he was doing, and she almost jumped out of her skin when a chord on a guitar was struck near her ear. She rolled protestingly on to her back, and then felt a reluctant surge of interest when she saw Dan seated with his back to the wheel strumming the instrument. His legs were crossed, one ankle resting on his knee, and the guitar was draped lazily across his thighs. As she continued to watch him he flicked a mocking glance in her direction before beginning to play a taunting Country and Western tune, the lyrics of which were in no way complimentary to an independent woman.

'Do you sing, too?' she enquired, propping herself up on her elbows, and as if in answer he changed to an instrumental that had topped the singles charts some weeks before.

With a sigh, Julie sat up, crossing her legs and facing him with some impatience. 'All right, you're good,' she said caustically. 'What is this—music to soothe the savage beast?'

'The word is breast,' he mocked, playing a final chord and putting the guitar aside. 'Music to soothe the savage breast! Which reminds me, there's another bikini below with both pieces intact.'

Julie's face burned, and she bent her head angrily, annoyed with her own inability to control her emotions where he was concerned. 'You know I'm wearing the briefs,' she told him moodily. 'I—I just didn't feel like—like making an exhibition of myself, that's all.'

Dan shrugged and stood up, but although she felt a moment's apprehension he only stepped over her legs again and went down the ladder, his bare feet soundless on the rubber-encased rings.

Her solitude destroyed, Julie decided to follow him, and found that they were approaching an island. There was a bay, set within the sheltering curve of the headland, and she gazed at it with undeniable interest as Dan handled the controls.

The powerful engines were slowed to a snail's pace, and the yacht moved slowly through the channel and into the bay. Then, some distance out from the sandy shore, he cut the engines altogether and dropped anchor, and the sudden silence was almost unnerving.

'Iroquois Bay,' he remarked, turning from the wheel and looking at her. 'The Huron Indians were practically wiped out by the Iroquois, even though they were both technically from the same linguistic family. But people are like that, aren't they? They always see enemies where there are none.'

'I imagine they had a reason,' replied Julie tautly, concentrating on the pine-covered slopes that climbed above the bay, and Dan inclined his head.

'Oh, sure. They were bitter enemies in the fur trade, but the Hurons were far the more civilised tribe. They made friends with the French, and the Jesuits made quite a number of converts. But the Iroquois were a bloodthirsty crew and I guess they didn't want to be civilised.'

Julie shrugged. 'Why are you telling me all this?'

He grinned. 'Just to prove that constant hostility prevents the development of a good relationship.' He made a final examination of the instrumentation, and then came aft to where a small dinghy was suspended just above the waterline. 'Now, do you want to swim ashore, or would you rather take the dinghy?'

Julie sighed. 'I'd rather not go ashore at all.' She examined the narrow watch on her wrist. 'It's almost noon. Oughtn't we to be turning back?'

Dan just gave her a resigned look and waited with folded arms for her to make her next move. It was obvious she was going to have to go ashore one way or the other, and with an impatient sound she said:

'I suppose we might as well use the dinghy.'

'Okay.'

He released the cradle and the small craft splashed down on to the water, bobbing about unsteadily on the swell, making Julie feeling slightly sick just watching it.

She refused to accept the offer of Dan's hand to get into

the boat, however. Touching him was apt to create difficulties she would rather avoid, so she lurched into the
dinghy with more determination than grace. She saw to her
relief that it had an outboard motor, and she waited impatiently for Dan to join her. The sooner they were ashore
the better, as far as she was concerned, and she concentrated on the island, trying not to think about the heav-
ing craft beneath her.

Dan climbed in easily, used to the unpredictability of
the boat, and leaning over, pulled the cord that started the
motor. It took a couple of jerks before it actually fired,
however, and by the time they started out towards the shore
Julie was feeling decidedly green.

'What's wrong?' Dan enquired, noticing her pale face.
'You're not feeling seasick, are you?' He grinned. 'You're
probably hungry. Did you have any breakfast this morning?'

'You have no sympathy, do you?' she choked, turning
away from him. 'No, as a matter of fact, I've had nothing
since last night, but don't let it worry you!'

Dan said nothing more, and a few minutes later the
dinghy grounded on the shingly shore. Julie got up at once,
eager to get out on to dry land, and in so doing lost her
balance. Her head was spinning, and groping helplessly for
the side, she tumbled out into the shallows. Her jeans were
soaked in seconds, and before she could pull herself up-
right Dan had vaulted out beside her and hauled her up
into his arms.

'Stupid,' he muttered, swinging her off her feet, and she
had no strength left to protest as he carried her up the
beach. He set her down on the sand some distance from
where he had beached the dinghy, then reached for the
fastening of her jeans as she lay weakly back on her elbows.

'What do you think you're doing?' she demanded in
horror, clutching at her waist, but he brushed her hands
aside.

'Hold still,' he said, compelling the zip down and releasing the metal button. 'You can't lie around in wet clothes, but I'll go get you a spare pair of mine if you're so desperate.'

Julie's lips quivered. 'You have no right——'

'Don't I?' he asked, looking at her quizzically, and she had to tear her gaze away before she permitted something irrevocable to happen.

In actual fact, his hands on her body were a pleasurable experience, but she wondered bitterly how many girls he had undressed in this way. He was certainly adept at it, although perhaps she was being unjust. Jeans were jeans, no matter who was wearing them.

With the jeans removed, he stood up, looking down at her with disturbing eyes as he wrung them out. 'Well?' he said. 'How d'you feel? Do you want me to get you a sweater or something?'

'No.' Her eyes were sulky, and she was scooping-up handfuls of sand, allowing the grains to filter through her fingers. She knew it would be silly to get dressed again now. She was just beginning to feel cool, and he had seen her anyway. 'I'm all right. Go and do what you have to. I'm fine here.'

Dan grimaced. 'I don't have anything to do,' he told her patiently. 'Come and swim! The water's fine.'

'You swim,' she retorted, not looking at him. 'I want to sunbathe. Or at least, that's all I intend to do. Until it's time for us to go back.'

Dan sighed. 'Look, it's more sensible to swim on an empty stomach, and as we'll be having lunch in a half hour——'

'Will we?'

'Julie, don't bait me,' he warned, an edge sharpening his tone. 'Now, do you walk into the water unaided, or do I carry you?'

She was on her feet in a second, brushing the sand from

her thighs, gazing up at him in resentful silence, and with a shrug he left her. She watched him walk away, moving with the lithe fluidity that was so unusual in a man of his size and build, and her pulses quickened. There was a disruptive excitement in just being with him, she thought helplessly, but then she remembered Adam, and how concerned and angry he must be feeling, and the weakness left her.

She walked some distance along the beach before venturing into the water, but she might as well have saved herself the effort. Dan kept pace with her, several yards out from the shore, and when she waded into the water, he approached her with a purposeful crawl.

'Keep away from me!' she exclaimed, pursing her lips, but he only turned on to his back, kicking his legs lazily and making no attempt to do as she asked.

Shaking her head, she took the plunge, gulping as the cold water assaulted her overheated body. But it was delightful, and she couldn't remain angry for long when Dan started to fool around. He kept disappearing, surfacing right behind her so that she was startled into sudden flight. Then he would just sink below the waves for minutes at a time, and just as she was beginning to panic he would appear again, his grinning expression evidence of his awareness of her anxiety.

'Better?' he asked, turning on to his back beside her and kicking water over her, and after a moment she nodded.

'I suppose so.'

'Aren't you enjoying yourself?'

'Maybe,' she shrugged. 'But I shouldn't be.'

'Why not?' His eyes had darkened. 'No, don't answer that. I don't want to hear it.'

Julie sighed. 'Won't your—your aunt wonder where you are?' she ventured, and he grinned.

'She knows exactly where I am,' he stated dryly. 'Well,

maybe not the exact location, but she knows who I'm with.'

'How could she know that?' Julie frowned.

'Would you believe—I told her?'

'You mean—you mean——' Julie gazed at him incredulously. 'Why, you—you——'

'Race you to the shore!' he challenged laughingly, and needing something to expunge the frustration she was feeling, Julie lashed out at him angrily before threshing madly towards the beach.

She stumbled out on to the sand exhaustedly, and looked round for him with angry eyes. He was nowhere in sight, and she blinked and wrung out her hair, waiting for him to appear. He must have planned the whole trip, she thought resentfully, and if she could have handled the dinghy she would have set out for the yacht and left him to swim for it.

As the minutes passed, however, her anger quickly dissipated. Where was he? she wondered anxiously. Surely the blow she had delivered had not been that powerful. Even so, the doubts persisted, deepening as the water rippled shorewards without any sign of a swimmer's head.

'Dan!'

Her first attempt at calling his name was a tentative cry, barely reaching beyond the beach, and she repeated it a second and third time, projecting her voice a little further. Oh, please, she begged, let him be safe! She doubted she could bear it if anything had happened to him.

'Did I hear my name?'

The unexpected enquiry behind her brought her round with a start, her eyes widening in sudden relief at the sight of his familiar form. For a moment she gazed at him unguardedly, her feelings plain for anyone to see, and then anger banished all other emotions as she realised he had not *just* come out of the water.

'Where were you?' she gulped, her chin wobbling ignominiously, and he gestured back towards the rocky slopes above the beach.

'I just wanted to see if you'd miss me,' he remarked, grinning irrepressibly, and she swung her fist against his chest in angry retaliation.

'You let me think you'd drowned!' she accused him, unable to keep the tremor out of her voice and all the humour drained out of his face.

'Hey,' he exclaimed disbelievingly, 'you were really worried, weren't you?' He shook his head, taking hold of her by the shoulders and staring down at her. 'Julie—honey! I wouldn't frighten you deliberately. Hell, I'm sorry. I'm a louse! I don't deserve for you to be concerned about me.'

'No, you don't,' she concurred with a sniff, and with a muffled oath he pulled her into his arms, pressing her close to him, and burying his face in the hollow between her neck and her shoulder.

'I wouldn't hurt you, Julie,' he groaned, and she realised he had no idea how much he had done so already. But that was not his fault. It was hers—for allowing herself to fall in love with him.

'Did—did you say something about—about lunch?' she got out jerkily, as the compulsive warmth of his body began to penetrate hers, spreading tentacles of flame along her veins and weakening her already strained resistance, and he sighed. She thought at first he was going to ignore her, but after a moment he lifted his head and presently he drew back to look at her.

'Lunch,' he said, and his eyes were narrowed and softly caressing. 'Okay, let's have lunch. We have plenty of time, don't we?'

CHAPTER EIGHT

THEY ate on the yacht, though not in the cabin as Julie had expected. Dan installed her in a chair on the afterdeck, and then he went below to prepare the food. Julie felt a fraud, allowing him to do it, but she was not sufficiently familiar with him to insist on participating, and only when the delightful smell of grilling meat drifted up the steps did she venture to investigate.

Dan was at the stove, turning the succulent hamburger steaks on the grid, and there were sesame seed rolls and salad waiting on a tray. It made her realise how hungry she was, and by now completely at ease in the skimpy swim-suit, she crossed the floor to stand watching him.

'Forgiven me?' he asked, without looking at her, and she moved her shoulders in reluctant assent.

'Of course.'

'Of course?' His grey eyes met hers and she coloured.

'Something smells good,' she said evasively, and he turned back to what he was doing with more enthusiasm.

They ate lunch on the afterdeck, seated across from one another in the easy chairs, forking up pieces of steak and salad, munching on the sesame rolls. Dan had produced a bottle of red wine to drink with the meal and it added to the flavour of the meat. It also made Julie feel deliciously drowsy, and she relaxed completely under its influence. It was impossible to sustain hostilities anyway in such idyllic surroundings, the boat rocking gently on its mooring, the sky an arc of blue above. So they talked, about anything and everything, and Julie discovered what an entertaining companion Dan could be when she was not trading insults with him. He had been so many places and done so many interesting things, and she was fascinated by his stories of gold mining in South Africa and drilling for oil in the icy wastes of Alaska.

'My father believes it's important to know something of the real world before entering the cloistered halls of banking,' he explained, with a wry grimace. 'He says it's no use handling money if you have no conception how it's made. He thinks there are too many people in finance who come to it cold—straight from business school—without any background knowledge. Economists deal with paper assets, they handle millions of dollars, but it's only paper money. Even the gold standard is a man-made institution. Gold itself is worthless—it doesn't have the properties of uranium or the cutting power of a diamond. But in 1812 the U.K. adopted it as a monetary system, and since then it's achieved international status, but what does it really mean? In some countries the ordinary man in the street isn't allowed to own gold in any quantity, gold coins aren't used as currency any more, and even the standard itself is open to criticism. For one thing it makes it difficult for any single country to isolate its economy from depression or inflation in the rest of the world, and it's terribly easy to forget, when you're handling such enormous amounts of money, exactly whose sweat and toil have gone into making it.'

Julie smiled. 'So you did some sweating and toiling yourself?'

'You better believe it,' Dan grinned. 'I'm sorry if I'm boring you, but it's something I feel strongly about.'

'You're not boring me,' Julie protested vehemently. 'I'm fascinated, honestly. I didn't know there was so much to learn.'

'God!' Dan gave her an indulgent look. 'My father's going to love you. If he can get someone to listen to him, he's happy, and I don't know anyone who knows more about finance than he does.'

'Oh!'

Julie bent her head, disturbed by his careless statement. It was obvious he was speaking hypothetically. There was no earthly chance of her meeting his father, and she wished he had not said it. It destroyed the harmony they had achieved, and restored the obvious barriers between them.

'So, tell me about you,' he invited, after she had been silent for several minutes. 'Tell me how you've spent the last—what? Twenty years?'

'Twenty-two, actually,' admitted Julie in a low voice. 'Oh, I'm not very interesting, and I certainly haven't done any of the things you've done.'

'That's a relief,' he remarked dryly, and she felt a reluctant smile lifting her lips once again. 'Come on, Julie, tell me about your father. I want to know.'

Julie sighed. 'You said you knew ...'

'I've heard the story. But I want you to tell it, the way it is.'

Julie put down her wine glass and lay back in her seat, studying the ovals of her toenails. 'Well,' she said slowly, 'he shot himself. He put a gun in his mouth and shot himself. That's it.'

'No, it's not.' Dan was serious now, leaning forward in his seat, knees apart, hands hanging loosely between. 'I want to know what was behind it. Where you were at the time. And what Price's part in it all was.'

Julie hesitated. The mention of Adam's name had reminded her of where she was and to whom she was speaking, but Dan's earnest expression dispelled her momentary reluctance.

'All right,' she said. 'I was at school, at a finishing school in France, when it happened. Adam brought me home.'

'And before that?'

Julie licked her lips. 'Well, as you probably know, my father and Adam were partners in a law firm ...'

'Yes.'

'Daddy had originally been in partnership with the man who founded the firm, and when Mr Hollingsworth died Adam joined him. I suppose that was about—fifteen years ago now.'

'Go on.'

Julie frowned. 'Daddy used to deal with all the work concerning probate and the administration of deceased' estates. He handled clients' investments, trusts, that sort of thing. Anyway ...' She paused, composing her words carefully, 'when my mother was taken ill, there were apparently a lot of medical expenses. Daddy didn't have the money.' She took a deep breath. 'You don't need me to tell you what happened.'

'I guess he borrowed from clients' resources?'

'Not initially,' she confessed quietly. 'He—he borrowed what he could from the bank, and when that was overdrawn he went to a credit agency.'

'I see.'

Julie shook her head. 'I knew nothing about it, of course. I was only about seven at the time, and when Mummy died he sent me away to a convent school, and I only used to see him in the holidays, and not always then. It was Adam who came to speech days and sports days and replied to my letters.'

Dan hunched his shoulders. 'I guess that's what makes him think he has the right to look after you now.'

Julie shrugged. 'Adam was always very fond of me. Even when he and Daddy—what I mean is, he was always the same with me.' She caught her lower lip between her teeth. 'I think sometimes Daddy resented Adam's affection for me, but I don't think he really cared about anything after Mummy died,' she added, unable to disguise the break in her voice.

'Oh, honey ...' Dan stretched across the space between them and captured her hand in both of his. 'Was it very bad?' He shook his head. 'I didn't mean to upset you, I just wanted you to talk about it. To get it out of your system.'

Julie bent her head. 'I'll never do that.'

'Why not? It's over.' Dan squeezed her fingers until they hurt. 'Baby, believe me, you have your own life to lead now. The past is over. Dead! And you can't resurrect it.'

Julie's faint smile revealed her lack of conviction in this statement, and as if realising she was becoming too morose, Dan stood up and pulled her up with him.

'Come on,' he said, releasing her almost immediately. 'We'll load the dishes in the washer and then we'll go ashore again. Okay?'

Julie acquiesced, as much from a desire to dispel the mood of dejection which was gripping her as from any obligation to obey him. For the present he had successfully banished any inclination to return to the hotel. Adam was at the hotel, and right now Adam represented too many things she wanted to forget. She refused to consider the eventual outcome of this reckless abduction. She would face that when she had to, but for now she wanted fun and freedom and escape—though from what she hardly knew.

Dan took his guitar ashore, and she stretched lazily on a towel beside him, enjoying the undemanding refuge of his music. It was so easy to forget time and consequence lying there, to lose oneself in abstract pleasure, and exist only for the moment. The only intruders were the wild geese who considered these islands exclusively theirs, and who uttered their mournful protest as they rose gracefully into the air.

After a while Dan put the guitar aside and relaxed beside her, closing his eyes against the unrelenting glare of the sun. Julie, already sleepy, felt her eyes closing, and for a time there was utter silence.

Julie stirred first, her skin protesting against the unremitting heat, and leaving Dan lying on the sand, she went to submerge herself in the cooling waters of the lake. It was a delightful release, and when she walked back up the beach she felt better than she had done for weeks.

Dan was still asleep, flat on his back, one arm raised to protect his face. He looked young and disturbingly attractive, and Julie felt her senses stir just looking at him. This was what he would look like in the mornings, she thought, picturing him in bed, in *her* bed, and she wrapped her arms about herself tightly, as if to ward off the dangers he represented.

But after a few moments she realised the futility of that and sank down beside him. Crossing her legs, she adjusted them to the lotus position, and then unwound herself again and rested back on her elbows. She was restless, and almost compulsively her gaze turned in Dan's direction.

The uplift of his arm had shifted the waistband of his shorts lower on his stomach, and she noticed how well the cuffs fitted his brown legs. They might have been made for him, she reflected reluctantly, her eyes moving up over the flat stomach to the waistband once more. There was a darker mark on his stomach, she noticed now, and leaning forward she realised it was the start of his scar. Although it had healed, there was still a puckering of the flesh around it, and her fingers moved almost involuntarily towards it, curious to see more.

'I said I'd show you if you wanted to see it,' Dan remarked huskily, and her hand was withdrawn without making contact.

'I—I was curious, that's all,' she explained, embarrassed at being caught out, but he only pushed the waistband lower until she could see the whole of the scar and the arrowing of hair below his navel.

'Ugly, isn't it?' he observed with a grimace. 'Scarred for life!'

Julie dragged her horrified gaze away, seeking the lazy indulgence of his, and his fingers reached up to curve around her nape, under the weight of her hair.

'Don't look so worried,' he taunted gently. 'It doesn't hurt. It's six or seven weeks since it happened. I'm not about to break open, you know.'

Julie shivered, but her eyes drifted irresistibly back to the scar. Then, almost involuntarily, she bent and put her lips to the narrow ridge of hard tissue than ran diagonally across his body, and felt his convulsive response.

'Julie,' he groaned, grasping a handful of her hair, and hauling her head painfully up to his. 'Julie, have some sense!' he muttered hoarsely, but right then she didn't feel particularly sensible. His lips parted almost tentatively beneath the tremulous exploration of her mouth, and she knew this was what she had been waiting for.

It wasn't enough just to look at Dan. She wanted to touch him. She wanted him to touch her. And there was an aching need inside her that she sensed only he could fulfil. She wanted to be close to him like this, closer than even his shorts or her bikini would allow, and her legs curled seductively between his, unconsciously alluring in her search for satisfaction.

'God, Julie,' he muttered, rolling her over on to her back and covering her damp body with his. 'Let me go and cool off in the water or I won't be responsible for the consequences.'

'Isn't it good?' she breathed, her silky arms entwined around his neck, and he took possession of her mouth with hard urgency before pressing himself away from her.

She watched him plunge into the lake, the ripples his entry made spreading unevenly along the sand. He wasn't visible for several seconds, but when he did emerge, he was several yards out from the shore, swimming strongly against the current.

With a sigh Julie sat up, realising dully that already the sun was sinking in the west, and soon they would have to go back. This had been a day out of time, but it was almost over, and in a very short while she would have to see Adam and explain where she had been and why. Tomorrow she was leaving, and eventually she would have to go back to England and the trailing threads of the life she had left behind. There was no point in railing against an established fact. It was there. It was irrevocable. And she had to accept it.

She had gathered the towels and Dan's guitar into the dinghy by the time he returned, and he gave himself a quick rub down before piloting them back to the yacht. Once on board she expected him to start the powerful engines, but he didn't, he went below, and she fretted about on deck waiting for him to reappear.

He didn't, however, and beginning to feel slightly chilled in her damp bikini, she ventured down the steps. To her astonishment, she found Dan heating soup on the stove, dressed now in the jeans and sweatshirt he had been wearing earlier. He was aware of her approach, and noticing the goosebumps on her skin, he said:

'If you're cold, get dressed. The soup won't be long.'

She hesitated, tempted to ask when they were leaving, and then bit on her tongue. She would know soon enough, and the idea of getting dressed and sharing a bowl of soup with Dan was too attractive a prospect to spoil.

She found her shirt and jeans in the cabin where she had left them, and quickly towelled herself completely dry. Her hair was still damp, of course, but she secured it with a piece of string she found in one of the drawers, and emerged feeling infinitely warmer.

Dan had laid two places on the table in the cabin, and she paused a moment to admire the silver cutlery and slim crystal glasses. Everything was suited to its surroundings, she thought, not least Dan himself.

As well as the soup, there was some cold ham and potato chips, or crisps, as Julie was used to calling them. There were more of the sesame rolls, and a bowl of salad, and another bottle of wine, white this time.

'It will be dark soon,' she ventured, as he joined her on the banquette, and he nodded his head. Since that disturbing moment on the beach he had said almost nothing to her, and her skin prickled at the awareness of feelings suppressed.

'Have some wine,' he said, uncorking the bottle, and she held the delicate glass for him to fill. 'It's hock,' he added, as her tongue circled her lips in anticipation, and her eyes smiled at him across the rim as she tasted its slightly dry flavour.

'It's delicious,' she averred, in answer to his unspoken question. 'But so was the wine at lunchtime,' She paused. 'Everything's been—wonderful.'

Dan averted his gaze and concentrated on spooning soup into his mouth, and Julie put her glass down and applied herself to the food. She was hungry, but the prospect of what was ahead of her tended to inhibit her appetite, and after a few spoonfuls she had had enough.

If Dan noticed that her dish was almost full when he returned it to the sink, he said nothing, and she endeavoured to make a better effort with the ham. But it was no good. Her throat seemed to close up every time she allowed herself to think that this time tomorrow she would be aboard the 747, and she pushed her plate aside with a feeling of desperation.

'Don't you like it, or aren't you hungry?' Dan enquired at last, and she gave him a sideways look before getting up from the banquette and wandering aimlessly round the cabin.

'We ought to be going back,' she said, gripping the edge of the sink and staring broodingly through the porthole at the rocky headland. It wasn't what she wanted to say, but it had to be said, and maybe she would find it easier once it was over. 'We have a long way to go, don't we?'

There was silence for a few minutes, and then Dan said quietly: 'Are you so desperate to leave me?'

Julie swung round, still holding on to the sink behind her. 'That's not the point, is it?' she demanded, her face flushed. 'Oh, I know I haven't any room for complaint regarding your behaviour. Apart from the fact that you tricked me into coming with you, you—you've behaved commendably. I know I haven't. But you—I've never denied I find you—attractive.'

'Oh, Julie ...' Dan spoke slowly, shaking his head as he did so. 'Stop trying to find excuses. We're good together, we knew that before today.' He regarded her with lazy indulgence. 'But it's more, isn't it? I think we both know that today can't end. Not in the way you're envisaging anyway.'

Julie stared at him, her lips parting anxiously, and he got up from the banquette and came towards her. His feet were bare, but he was still several inches taller than she was, and in the lengthening shadows of the cabin he seemed absurdly menacing.

'Dan ...' she murmured, putting out a hand as if to ward him off, but he just used it to pull her towards him, hauling her close into his arms. 'Dan, don't touch me ...'

'Touch you?' he groaned, burying his face in her hair. 'Julie, I've got to touch you. I've got to hold you.' He lifted his head to look down at her. 'I love you, Julie, I love you!'

'You—love—me?'

It was a disbelieving squeak, and for a moment, humour deepened the lines beside his eyes. 'Yes, I love you,' he repeated, probing the contours of her lips with his thumb. 'I love you, and I want to make love to you.' His eyes darkened passionately. 'I want to be part of you, Julie. Don't tell me you don't want that too.'

His husky confession had left her weak and confused and totally incapable of fighting him. When his mouth found hers with sensual sureness, she could only cling to him urgently, returning his kisses in helpless abandon. All day she had been aware of the tumultuous craving inside her, and his lips ignited the flame she had tried to subdue. Re-

leased from the bonds of inhibition, it burned like a forest
fire, eating away her resistance, engulfing her in a blaze of
passion. If Dan had had any doubt about her feelings, they
were consumed by the eager submission of silken arms and
seeking lips, and his own emotions ran wildly in concert
with hers.

Swinging her off her feet, he carried her through the
twin-bedded cabin to the double bunk in the master cabin.
With his mouth still clinging to hers, he deposited her on
the damask cover and subsided on top of her, the muscular
weight of his body a potent intoxicant to her already en-
flamed senses.

Kisses were rapidly becoming not enough, and with a
groan he drew back to tug the sweatshirt over his head, ex-
posing the brown expanse of his chest. Then, when his
fingers would have gone to the belt of his jeans, she forestalled him, unfastening the buckle herself, holding his eyes
with hers as she did so.

'Julie,' he moaned, half in protest, but she seemed to
know instinctively how to please him, and pleasure over-
came all else.

With quickening passion Dan undressed her, his mouth
hard and persuasive on hers when she felt the muscled
hardness of him against her for the first time. It was a disturbing experience, but wonderfully satisfying, though her
face flamed when he drew back to look at her.

'Don't be shy,' he said huskily, when she withdrew her
arm from around his neck to cover herself. 'We have no
secrets from one another. And you're much better to look at
than I am.'

'I—I wouldn't say that,' she breathed, drawing his mouth
back to hers, and he crushed her beneath him as the
urgency of his own needs made anything else impossible.

It was odd, but she wasn't afraid.

Years ago, in the convent, when she had heard girls
whispering about the things that happened between a man

and a woman, she had been. Even the practicality of biology lessons had not persuaded her that anyone could find enjoyment in such pursuits, and she had determinedly put such thoughts from her mind.

Even later, at the finishing school in France, she had felt apprehensive of that side of marriage, but Adam had always been so retiring in terms of a physical relationship that she had assumed she would get used to it when she had to.

But since meeting Dan, all those preconceived notions had gone out the window. She had suspected from the first time he held her in his arms that a girl might feel differently with him, and she was right. Being close to somebody, becoming a part of him, was not something one contrived. With the right person, it was a natural extension of their love for one another, and with Dan she wanted to experience everything. It wasn't enough to lie in his arms—she needed to know all there was to know about him ...

It happened so naturally that afterwards she scarcely remembered the sharp stab of pain that heralded his invasion of her innocence. The sensual possession of his lips left her weak with longing, and she instinctively arched herself against him, inviting the penetrating thrust of his body.

But even then, she had had no conception of how it might be. Her timid expectations had been limited by a physical reality, and she had had no idea of the sensations Dan could arouse inside her. She had wanted to please him, to give him pleasure, to drive away the look of strain he had worn when he left her on the beach; but instead he was pleasuring her, exciting her, invoking feelings that demanded a full and consummate expression. When the crescendo began to build inside her, she heard the moans she was emitting and hardly recognised herself. Her nails were digging into Dan's shoulders, raking the smooth brown skin, and when the release came she would not let him go. Instead, she wound herself about him, her mouth clinging to his, and minutes sank into oblivion as the world slowly steadied and righted itself.

Dan lifted his head with reluctance some minutes later, his eyes still dark and glazed with emotion. He looked down at her intently, just visible in the fading light, and then he said huskily: 'It was good, wasn't it?'

Julie reached up to touch his cheek with her fingers, and when he turned his lips into her palm she whispered: 'I love you, Dan. But you know, don't you? I'm not very good at hiding my feelings.'

'Thank God for that!' he murmured fervently, and took possession of her mouth again, tenderly now, and eloquent with emotion.

Some minutes later he aroused himself sufficiently to add gently: 'In answer to your question, I did suspect you didn't altogether object to my attentions.' He gave a wry smile. 'Even though you have given me some bad moments.'

'I have?' She brushed the thick swathe of dark hair back from his forehead with soft fingers and he nodded.

'Like at the party, for instance,' he averred huskily. 'When Corinne broke in on us. I didn't sleep well last night, Julie. I didn't sleep well at all.'

'But you will tonight,' she murmured breathily, and he nodded.

'With you,' he said, his voice deepening. 'We'll go back in the morning, hmm? Then we'll tell them we're going to be married.'

'Married?' Julie gazed up at him.

'Don't sound so surprised,' he teased. 'Or have you had lots of lovers?'

She flushed. 'You know that's not true.'

'Mmm—mmm.' He grinned with satisfaction. Then he bent his head to kiss her once more. 'But you will marry me, won't you?' he breathed, against her lips. 'Just as soon as I can get a licence?'

Julie caught her breath. 'Oh, Dan, you know I want to, but——'

'But what?' He propped himself up on one elbow to look down at her. Then his expression hardened. 'Don't tell me you're still going to marry Price?'

'No.' She sighed. 'No, of course not——' She broke off as he stroked her lips with his tongue. 'But Dan, your aunt —your family——'

'—will love you as I do,' he interrupted her roughly, and there was silence for a while as he explored her mouth with his own. 'Julie, I've never asked any girl to marry me before. Don't tell me no.'

'Oh, I'm not,' she confessed eagerly. 'Of course I'll marry you, Dan. Tomorrow, if it was possible. Only—only please——'

'What?' His smoky eyes were narrowed.

'—make love to me again!' she finished huskily, and with a muffled groan, he complied.

They drank the remains of the wine at midnight, curled up in the comfortable double berth. They had had a shower together earlier, and now Julie was pleasantly sleepy and utterly at peace.

'I'm so glad you kidnapped me,' she murmured, burrowing against him, and Dan relaxed on his back, gazing contentedly up at the ceiling.

'You didn't think so this morning,' he mocked, slanting a look down at her, his expression indulgent in the mellow lamplight, and Julie pummelled her fists against him, pressing her nose against his chest.

'I guess I was afraid of you—or of myself,' she admitted soberly. 'I was afraid to get involved. I was afraid of being hurt.'

'And did I hurt you?' he asked, rolling over on to his stomach beside her, and she wound her arms around his neck.

'Some,' she confessed softly. 'Oh, Dan, this is real, isn't it? I'm not going to wake up and find it's all just a dream, am I?'

'Nope.' He stroked her hair back from her face with tender fingers. 'You're stuck with me,' he conceded gently. 'Now, do you want any more wine, or can I put out the light?'

'Put out the light,' repeated Julie happily. 'Hmm, that sounds nice. Put out the light, darling.'

Dan was not proof against such endearments, and in the ensuing darkness his mouth sought and found hers with increasing urgency.

CHAPTER NINE

THE radio telephone disturbed them at six in the morning.

Julie awakened from a sound slumber to find Dan already stirring, squinting at the dial of his watch with impatient eyes. It was already light outside, but the drawn curtains made the cabin shadowy, and it took some seconds for him to focus. Then he groaned as he pushed back the sheet that was all that covered them and thrust his long legs out of bed.

'What is it?' Julie asked drowsily, not recognising the distinctive buzz, and Dan paused a moment to bestow a warm kiss on her parted lips.

'Just the telephone,' he murmured, tucking the covers about her again and reaching for his jeans. 'I won't be long.'

She watched him walk through the cabin beyond to the living area, zipping himself into his jeans as he went, and a feeling of cold apprehension gripped her. She guessed only his family knew how to reach him, and her lips felt dry as she passed her tongue over them. After all, the Leytons must be wondering where Dan was and whether he was all right, and her conscience stung her at the realisation of how little thought she had given to whether anyone might be worried about her.

It seemed ages before he came back and by then she was sitting up in the middle of the wide mattress, the sheet tucked anxiously under her chin. With her silky hair loose about her shoulders, she was unknowingly provocative, and Dan's eyes darkened as they met the troubled depths of hers.

'Who was it?' she asked, gazing up at him, and unable to resist the artless temptation she represented, Dan sank down on to the bed and tugged the protective sheet aside.

'Would you believe—Aunt Anthea?' he murmured, against the creamy flesh of her breast, and she slid her fingers into his hair to pull his head back and look at him.

'Yes?'

Dan shrugged, his eyes drowsy with emotion. 'Can't it wait?' he suggested huskily, seeking the curve of her ear, and although she wanted to give in she had to know the worst.

'Dan, please . . .'

'Okay, okay.' He drew back from her completely and took a deep breath. 'Apparently your friend—friends—have been concerned about you.'

Julie's brows drew together. 'Do you mean Pam and David? Or Adam?'

Dan shrugged, his shoulders smooth and bronzed in the early morning light. 'I'd guess the latter, but I don't know.'

'So what happened?'

Dan sighed. 'Well, when you didn't get back by midnight, he—they—phoned Forest Bay.'

'Oh, *lord*!'

Dan shook his head. 'No sweat. Max told them you'd be okay with me.'

Julie could imagine how Adam—*how all of them*—would have taken that. 'Is that all?'

'No.' Dan pushed a weary hand into his hair. 'They phoned again around two a.m. and insisted Max got in touch with us—Brad must have told them about the radio link. But Max refused to phone at that hour of the night, so Anthea waited until it was light and—that's it.'

'Oh, Dan!' Julie sat cross-legged facing him, anxiety darkening her delicate features, like a slim naiad in the pale illumination filtering through the curtains, and she felt his senses stirring urgently. 'We must go back.'

'I know it,' he said huskily. But not yet. Not yet——'

It was a little after nine when the *Spirit of Atlantis* sailed in to the mooring below Kawana Point. Dan was seated at the wheel, with Julie on the seat beside him, her arm around his neck and looped to the other arm that circled his chest.

In spite of the apprehension she felt at seeing Adam again, she was supremely content in the knowledge of Dan's love for her, and he was already talking of taking her to New York to meet his parents. So far as he was concerned, he saw no reason why they shouldn't be married almost immediately. He didn't like bringing her back to the hotel, and he showed the first trace of anger towards her when, after he had manoeuvred the yacht into the marina, she said she would rather speak to Adam alone.

'Why?' he demanded, his expressive eyes steel grey in his tanned face, and she almost succumbed. He looked tired this morning, she thought, smoothing back the hair from his temple, and then smiled when she recalled the cause of his weariness. 'What's so funny?' he added harshly, his hands hard on her hips, and she quickly put her fingers across his lips.

'Darling, I was just thinking how handsome your haggard look is,' she protested, evading his urgent response. 'When will I see you again? Later this morning? This afternoon?'

Dan sighed. 'You'd better make it this afternoon,' he said heavily, 'if you insist on going through with this alone. I'll spend the time making the arrangements for our trip to New York. I guess you don't have a visa, do you?'

Julie shook her head, and with a groan he gathered her close to him again. 'You won't let Price change your mind, will you?' he muttered. 'I think I'd go out of my mind if you left me now.'

'Oh, Dan ...' Julie's voice was shaken, too. 'These last twenty-four hours have been the most wonderful in my life! I love you. How could I change that?'

Dan let her go unwillingly, retaining a hold on her hand as she prepared to step ashore. 'I'll come by after lunch,' he said. 'We'll spend the afternoon on the lake. At least that way I can be sure of having you all to myself.'

Julie glanced at him adoringly, aware of the meaning behind those simple words, and he took the opportunity to kiss her once again. 'I love you,' he said, in a strangled tone, and then turned away as she stepped on to the jetty.

Julie guessed the yacht had been sighted coming into the marina, but there was no one to meet her. She did gain a casual salutation here and there from the yachtsmen who were staying at the hotel and who were down attending to their craft, but there was no sign of David or Adam, and Pam was no doubt involved with her regular morning routine.

She was halfway up the steps when she saw Brad lounging at the top of the flight waiting for her. He was propped against the rail, and as she came abreast of him he offered her an awkward grin.

'Hi!'

'Hi,' she answered, glad to break the ice with him. 'Isn't it a lovely——'

'Mr Price is real mad with you!' the boy broke in urgently. 'And Mom and Dad, too. Where've you been? Did you spend the night on the yacht?'

Julie sighed. 'Yes.'

'With Dan?'

'Yes.'

'Gosh!' Brad shook his head at this, and she realised that for the moment he was more envious of her good fortune than anything else. 'I bet that was terrific!'

Julie smiled. 'It was rather.'

Brad gazed at her admiringly, then shoved his hands into the pockets of his jeans. 'You know, I'd really like to do that,' he exclaimed, entirely diverted now at the prospect. 'I've never slept on board a boat before. Did you have meals, too? There's a proper stove, isn't there, and a refrigerator——'

'That's enough, Brad!' David's brusque tones interrupted them, and Julie saw that Pam's husband had approached them without either of them being aware of it. 'Go find Pietro. Tell him I want some more cases of beer up from the cellar.'

Julie stopped Brad, however, before he could dart away, taking hold of his firm young arm and saying gently: 'You know, I might be able to arrange something, about the yacht, I mean. If your parents don't object.'

Brad gulped. 'Hey, do you mean it?'

'I said that's enough, Brad,' David intervened once again. 'There'll be no yachting trips for you. Julie's going away. She won't be able to arrange anything.'

Julie let the boy go, as much to save him the humiliation of arguing with his father as through any desire to protect him from what she had to say. But as he charged away across the square she turned to David fearlessly and in cutting tones she said:

'I think you've got it wrong, David. I shan't be leaving, after all. Not crossing the Rockies, anyway. I'm going to marry Dan Prescott.'

David could not have looked more stunned, but he recovered quickly, and gave an impatient shrug. 'Perhaps you ought to wait and see what Adam has to say about that,' he muttered, indicating the hotel behind them. 'Come along. He's in the apartment. He's waiting to speak with you.'

Julie sighed. 'He won't make me change my mind, David. It's quite made up already. And nothing he—or any of you—can say will alter it.'

Pam met them in the reception hall, her face flushed from the kitchen, and she avoided her husband's eyes as she asked if Julie was all right.

'I'm fine.' Julie returned the kiss the other girl offered her with warmth. 'Honestly, Pam,' she insisted, looking compassionately at her friend. 'I've never been so happy in my life.'

'What—what do you———'

'Don't you think we ought to be saying all this in front of Adam?' David suggested curtly, gesturing towards the door to their apartment. 'He is most involved, isn't he?'

'I just wanted to———'

'I think you've done enough, Pamela,' her husband cut in coldly. 'If you hadn't filled Julie's head———'

'No, that's not true!' Julie couldn't let Pam take the blame. 'David, I was attracted to Dan from the minute I first saw him. He knew that, and so did I. I've just been—fighting it, that's all.'

'You mean—he cares about you?' Pam stared at her in astonishment, and Julie nodded.

'He wants to marry me,' she said gently. 'Honestly. We're going to New York tomorrow or the day after so that I can meet his parents.'

'Oh, Julie!'

Pam was obviously overcome, but her husband only flung open their living room door and urged both girls inside without making any comment. His face was grim, and Julie passed him with a feeling of resignation.

Adam was standing by the window, staring out broodingly at the tennis courts where a good-natured mixed doubles was taking place amid gales of laughter. He turned at their entrance, however, and the pitying expression on his face aroused a curious fluttery feeling inside her. In a light grey lounge suit, he looked austere after the casual attire normally worn around the hotel, and she dropped the jacket she was carrying, deciding it didn't really matter what he thought of her shirt and jeans now.

'Good morning, Julie,' he greeted her, almost as if he hadn't been up half the night trying to discover her whereabouts. 'I'm pleased to see you're obviously unharmed.'

His severe tone made David shift awkwardly from one foot to the other, and after giving Julie an assessing look he turned to his wife. 'I think we ought to leave them to it,

Pam,' he said abruptly. 'After all, now that we know Julie's safe, it's really not our affair.'

Pam looked reluctant to leave and truthfully Julie would have been glad of her support, but she could see how difficult it was for them, and with a smile she said:

'I'll see you later, Pam. We can talk then.'

'All right.' Pam made an offhand movement of her shoulders. 'If—er—if you need me, Julie, just give a call.'

Julie appreciated the gesture, and after they had gone she sought refuge in helping herself to some coffee from the tray on the bureau. Then, when it was impossible to continue avoiding the inevitable, she said:

'I'm sorry, Adam. I'm sorry you were worried about me, and I'm sorry this had to happen.'

Adam folded his hands behind his back. 'Brad told us where you'd gone, of course.'

'I guessed he would.' Julie took a nervous mouthful of her coffee. 'I'm sorry.'

Adam shrugged, apparently as calm and unflappable as ever. 'It's over now. I just hope it's brought you to your senses.'

Julie's cup clattered on to the tray. 'What do you mean?'

'Isn't it obvious?' Adam spread an expressive hand. 'I'm not naïve, Julie. I can see what's happened between you two. And I can't deny a certain amount of—irritation, that things had to go so far. But,' he hastened on as she would have interrupted him, 'perhaps you needed the experience. Perhaps you needed to be brought face to face with reality. Obviously, my words on the matter had little effect, but it must be apparent to you now the kind of man you're dealing with——'

'Adam, it wasn't—it *isn't*—like that!' Julie tried to explain. 'We—we love one another, Dan and I. He—he wants to marry me.'

'Oh, does he?' Adam did not sound at all surprised, and Julie wondered with a sense of bafflement what she had to say to disconcert him. 'And what does his family have to say about that?'

'I—we—don't know, do we?' Julie shook her head. 'I'm sorry, Adam. I know this must come as a great shock to you, but I—I am going to marry him. I'm going to meet his parents within the next few days.'

'Really?' Adam's lip curled. 'I shouldn't be too hopeful of that, if I were you.'

'Why not?' Julie stared at him.

'Simply that Anthea Leyton assured me last night that there was not the slightest chance of Dan marrying anyone but his cousin. His *step*-cousin, that is. Corinne. You may remember, you met her at——'

'Dan's not going to marry Corinne!' Julie's tone rang with conviction. 'Why, he doesn't even like her!'

'Liking is not a necessary attribute to marriage,' retorted Adam calmly. 'Suitability; convenience; *expediency*. These are the factors people like the Prescotts and the Leytons take into account.'

Julie squared her shoulders. 'You're wrong.'

'I know these people, Julie.'

'Well, even if you're right about what Anthea Leyton told you, you're wrong about Dan and me.' Julie took a deep breath. 'I realise this must be distressing for you, Adam, but you wouldn't want to marry me, would you, knowing I loved someone else?'

Adam hesitated, his brows drawing together across the narrow bridge of his nose. Then he came towards her. 'Julie,' he said, placing his hands on her shoulders, 'I know how you feel, believe me. And I believe you when you say you love this man. But he's not worthy of you——'

'Don't say that.' Julie twisted away from him. 'Dan's the most marvellous—the most sensitive man I've ever known.'

'And how many men have you known, Julie?' asked Adam quietly. 'A handful, that's all.'

'You expected me to marry you, knowing the same,' she countered, and Adam sighed.

'How long have we known one another, Julie? Fifteen years? A little different from three—maybe four weeks, isn't it?'

'I know Dan,' she insisted.

'You know what he's told you,' corrected Adam evenly. 'You don't know his home, his background——'

'I intend to.'

'And this is what he intends as well?'

'Yes.'

Adam shook his head. 'You know what I think? I think he realised the kind of—fanciful, romantic girl you are. I think he knew that you'd never agree to an—affair. There had to be something more. Something concrete, for you to build your hopes and dreams upon. So he came up with this idea of marriage——'

'That's not true!' Julie's eyes were wide and indignant. 'You don't know how it was. You have no idea. If—if Dan had wanted an affair, he—he could have had one.'

Adam's lips thinned. 'What are you saying?'

Julie flushed. 'I'm saying that—that it was—Dan who held back.' She sighed. 'And he didn't ask me to marry him—before. It was after.'

Adam showed the first signs of crumbling dignity. 'You don't expect me to believe that?'

'It's the truth.' Julie pressed her palms together. 'Oh, Adam, I don't want to hurt you. I don't want to lose your friendship, but you have to believe this is the most wonderful thing that's ever happened to me.'

'And what about his feelings when he discovers your father took his own life?'

Julie bent her head. 'He knows.'

'He knows?'

'Yes. I told him.'

'I see.' Adam was finding it difficult now to maintain his

air of detachment. 'But no one else knows, do they? Not his aunt and uncle, or his parents?'

'I suppose not.' Julie felt a faint twinge of unease. 'But if Dan doesn't care——'

'Oh, Julie ...' Adam seemed to recover a little of his composure. 'What an innocent you are, aren't you?'

There was nothing to say to that, and with a helpless movement of her shoulders she would have left him then had not Adam chosen to ask one last question.

'Your plans?' he said. 'Am I permitted to know what you intend to do now?'

Julie turned, her tongue moistening her upper lip. 'Dan's coming back this afternoon. He—well, he's making arrangements for us to fly to New York, so that I can meet his parents.'

'I see,' Adam nodded. 'This afternoon. Very well, I'll delay making any decision about my own arrangements until tomorrow.'

Julie didn't know why, but she was apprehensive of his concern for her. It was as if his concern weakened her belief in what Dan had told her, and she didn't want to feel this sense of marking time.

'There's no need,' she said now, forcing a note of lightness into her voice. 'I—we—we'll probably be leaving for New York tomorrow. There's no need for you to delay your trip because of me.'

'But I want to,' said Adam firmly. 'It occurs to me that Prescott might well be leaving for New York tomorrow. But whether you will be with him or not ...'

Julie didn't wait to hear the end of his supposition. Snatching up her jacket, she left the room and stood for several seconds in the hall outside, trying to recover the feeling of conviction she had had when she came here.

Pam was looking out for her when she crossed the reception hall, and realising she owed it to her friend to explain, Julie followed her into the almost empty dining room.

'I've caused a lot of trouble, haven't I?' she said ruefully. 'Is David very angry?'

Pam grimaced. 'He's just suspicious-minded,' she declared, drawing Julie down into the chair opposite. 'Now, tell me: has Dan really asked you to marry him?'

'Really,' said Julie, and wondered why it didn't sound as convincing as it had before. 'Is that so unbelievable?'

'No.' Pam sounded defensive. 'Why should it be?'

'Oh, I don't know ...' Julie propped her head on her knuckles. 'Adam seems to think so.'

'Well, he would, wouldn't he?' suggested Pam reasonably. 'Mind you, I don't think he was so sure of himself last night.'

'No?'

'No.' Pam shook her head. 'We think he thought you might have eloped together. He was pretty sick, I can tell you.'

'Sick?' Julie stared at her friend. 'I can't believe it.'

'I know. He seems so emotionless, doesn't he? But you know, there are emotions there—beneath the surface.' Pam hesitated. 'Quite honestly, Julie, I'm glad you're not going to marry him——'

'Because he's too old—I know!' Julie humoured her, but Pam gestured her into an unwilling silence.

'No,' the older girl insisted, 'it's something else. Something I can't really explain. A—a kind of—gut feeling.'

'Oh, Pam!'

'No, listen to me. I know what I'm talking about. I don't think your Mr Price is half as—as nice as you think he is.'

'Pam, he's been like a father to me——'

'That's just it.' Pam pressed her palms on the table. 'He's like a father, but he's not. He wants you, Julie——'

'I know that.'

'—and I think he means to have you, no matter what.'

'Oh, honestly!' Julie was staring at her friend impatiently now. 'You're letting your imagination run away with you, Pam. Of course Adam wants me. He hasn't made a secret of it.'

'And did your father approve?' asked Pam urgently, then put her hand across the table to grip Julie's arm sympathetically. 'I'm sorry. I shouldn't have asked that.'

'Why not?' Julie looked at her squarely. 'I can talk about it now. I—Dan asked me about it, and I told him.'

'That's good.' Pam was approving. 'So—did your father want you to marry Adam?'

Julie hesitated. 'I think so. He never said he didn't.'

'But did you discuss it?'

'No—o.' Julie was trying to remember what her father had said about Adam. 'I think he just took it for granted. As Adam did—as *I* did.'

'Mmm.' Pam sounded thoughtful. 'I wonder.'

'What do you wonder?'

Pam shrugged. 'I'm not sure. I just wish your father was still alive, that's all.'

'So do I!' Julie spoke fervently, and for a few moments there was silence between them.

They were still sitting there, each involved with their own thoughts, when David came striding into the room. His square-cut features were set in dour lines, but they lightened somewhat when he saw Julie.

'The phone,' he said brusquely, approaching their table. 'You're wanted on the phone, Julie. I think it's Prescott.'

'Oh!' Julie sprang up from her seat and stood for a moment looking at him. 'I—where can I take it?'

'Go into the office,' directed David shortly. 'I'll wait here until you're finished.'

'Thanks.'

With an apologetic smile that encompassed both of them, Julie fled across the dining room, hurrying into the small office and closing the door firmly behind her. Then, controlling the unsteady tremor of her hand, she lifted the receiver David had left lying on his desk.

'H-hello?'

'Julie!'

Dan's voice was so endearingly familiar that she sank down weakly on to a corner of the desk, grasping the receiver tightly in her fingers. 'Dan? Oh, Dan, I'm so glad you called!'

'Why? What's wrong?' Almost intuitively he sensed her anxiety, and she had to force herself not to blurt the whole story of the morning's events into his waiting ear. It could wait until later. He had not rung to hear her troubles—particularly not when she had prevented him from accompanying her.

'Oh, nothing,' she managed now, hiding the tension she was feeling. 'W-why did you ring?'

'Would you believe to hear your voice?' he asked huskily, and when she didn't immediately respond he added: 'No, actually, it wasn't just for that. Julie, I've got to leave for New York this afternoon. I won't be able to keep our date after all.'

Julie heard what he had to say, but she couldn't believe it. Dan? Leaving for New York? Without her? There had to be some mistake. But there wasn't. The words had been said, and everything Adam had hinted washed over her in humiliating detail.

'Julie? Julie, did you hear what I said?'

She heard his words through the mists of disbelief, and realising he must never know the blow he had dealt her, she summoned all her fortitude to say: 'I heard.'

'Julie!' Dan's voice was low now, and filled with the impatience she remembered so well. 'You don't imagine I planned this, do you?'

Julie took a deep breath. 'P-planned what?' she got out jerkily, and heard the oath he muttered half under his breath.

'Julie, my father is not well. I *have* to go, do you understand? It's not a social visit.'

His father was *ill*? Julie absorbed this without conviction. She could imagine Adam's reaction to that. And why not? It had certainly come at a most convenient time.

'I'm sorry,' she said now, stiffly, but she sensed he was not satisfied with her answer and his next words confirmed it.

'What has Price been saying to you?' he demanded. 'I knew he'd try to poison your mind against me. You don't believe me, do you? You think this is some clever ploy arranged by my aunt and my father to get me away from Forest Bay, from the lake, from *you*!'

'And isn't it?'

Julie heard herself asking the words and heard his angry denial. 'No, goddammit,' he snapped. 'I wouldn't do that. I love you, Julie. But I can't help wondering what kind of love you feel for me that can be put in jeopardy with so little provocation!'

Julie gasped. 'That's not fair——'

'And is it fair to convict me without any evidence? To take another man's word before mine?'

'No, but——'

'Either you believe me or you don't.'

'Dan, Adam says you're going to marry Corinne.'

'Do you believe it?'

'I ... I didn't ...'

'Past tense?'

'I want to believe you, Dan.'

'Then do it.' He sighed. 'Julie, this is a hell of a time to do this to me!'

'Oh, Dan ...'

'I have to go. I'm flying from Barrie in less than an hour to connect with a flight from Toronto to Kennedy airport in New York, and I don't have time to come see you.'

'It's all right.' Somehow Julie managed to squash her

fears. 'I—when will you be back?'

'Tomorrow, the day after—how can I be sure!' Dan sounded distrait. 'Wait for me, Julie. Don't let anyone persuade you otherwise. Promise me!'

Julie licked her dry lips. 'I—I'll wait,' she agreed huskily. 'I'll wait. But please—don't make me wait too long ...'

Putting down the receiver was the hardest thing she had ever done, and even after the bell had rung signifying the connection had been broken, she sat for several minutes more just staring at the grey instrument. Then, when it became obvious that she couldn't stay in David's office any longer, she rose from the desk and let herself out of the room.

She didn't want to have to explain what had happened to Pam, but she had no alternative. The Galloways were waiting to hear what Dan had had to say, and she couldn't avoid the inevitable. However, she refused to let them see how shattered she was feeling, and she adopted a confident manner as she rejoined them in the restaurant.

'Dan's father's been taken ill,' she exclaimed, assuming an anxious tone. 'Isn't that a shame? Just at this time. Dan's terribly upset.'

Pam exchanged a glance with her husband, then said sympathetically: 'What rotten luck! Is it serious? Does this mean you won't be going to New York after all?'

Belatedly, Julie remembered she had not asked exactly what was wrong with Lionel Prescott, and flushing a little she avoided a direct answer. 'I shan't be going to New York,' she replied, endeavouring to keep her tone light. 'Not yet, anyway. Dan has to go, of course. It is his father, after all.'

'Of course,' echoed Pam, but there was another of those significant exchanges with her husband, which Julie recognised as a plea for sympathy. 'Oh, well ...' she continued. 'That means we'll be able to keep you for a little bit longer, doesn't it?'

It was Adam Julie dreaded to face, and the encounter came at lunchtime. She had had to go into the dining room to take her meal. Anything else would have prompted the suspicion that all was not as it should be, and she wanted to allay those kind of doubts. So she took her seat as usual, ordered an omelette and a side salad, then started nervously when Adam came to take the seat opposite.

'You don't mind if I join you, do you, Julie?' he enquired, pulling out the chair, and she shook her head quickly as he sat down. 'So,' he went on, 'they tell me the spare ribs are very good here. What would you recommend?'

Julie shrugged. 'I don't know your preference, do I?' she returned shortly.

'I think you do,' he averred, but he let it go. 'What have you ordered? Perhaps our tastes concur.'

'I'm just having an omelette,' said Julie, shaking out her napkin. 'And I know you don't like them.'

'Ah, you know so much about me, don't you, Julie?' he remarked, leaning back in his chair. 'My tastes in food, in clothes, in hotels—in women——'

'Please, Adam——'

'—and I know you,' he finished dryly. 'I know when you're happy and sad, when you're worried and anxious, or when you're apprehensive, like now, aware that I predicted exactly what Prescott would do!'

'Adam——'

'What's the matter, Julie? Can't we talk any more? Can't you confide in me? You always have. And I've always respected those confidences. Why is it suddenly so hard for you to discuss your problems with me?'

'You know why, Adam.'

'Because of Prescott? Why should that be so?'

'You're biased, Adam.'

'Am I? Well, perhaps a little. But if I thought he was the right man for you, do you think I'd stand in your way?'

Julie bent her head. 'I'd really rather not talk about it.'

'Why not? Because you suspect I'm right, and you're afraid to accept the truth?'

'*No!*' Julie lifted her head to look at him. 'Adam, Dan loves me, I *know* he does.'

'But he's gone away.'

'How do you know that?'

Adam shrugged. 'I could say your face says it all. But I won't. I'll admit, I asked Galloway.'

Julie sighed. 'Adam, Dan has gone to see his father who is unwell, that's all. He'll be back tomorrow, so you have no need to concern yourself about me.'

'Oh, but I do, Julie.' He toyed thoughtfully with the knife beside his plate. 'You see, I know a little more about the Prescotts than you do, and I also happen to know that Anthea Leyton was speaking to her brother yesterday on the phone, and he was perfectly healthy then.'

Julie had expected him to say something like this, so she was prepared for it, but that didn't prevent the twisting pain that tore into her heart at this news. Adam would say anything to make her believe the worst of Dan, she told herself fiercely, but it still hurt.

'Look,' she said, trying to speak slowly and succinctly, 'I'm not a fool. I know that this—this marriage—is going to cause problems. We both—Dan and I, that is—know that. But if we love one another——'

'You're a romantic, Julie,' exclaimed Adam scornfully. 'My God, I'm beginning to wonder if I ever knew you. I thought you were a sane and sensible girl, not a sentimental fool with her head filled full of pipe-dreams! Come down to earth, Julie. It's money that makes the world go round, not *love*, and the sooner you realise that the less painful it's going to be for you.'

The arrival of the waitress with Julie's omelette interrupted his remonstration, and Adam hastily ordered a steak to get rid of her. But to Julie's relief, Pam had noticed her flushed cheeks, and ignoring Adam's sour look of disapproval, she carried a cup of coffee to their table and sat down.

'Can I join you?' she asked, fanning herself energetically. 'I've been run off my feet since breakfast, and I must sit down or I'll collapse!'

CHAPTER TEN

THE rest of the meal passed without incident, Pam's presence preventing any serious conversation. Adam hardly spoke at all, except when Pam addressed him directly, and Julie was grateful for the other girl's perception. She had a lot to thank the Galloways for, she thought ruefully, but she couldn't help wondering whether she would always feel that way. If Dan let her down ...

But she refused to allow such negative thinking to ruin the day. Nothing had changed. She was still the same girl, and Georgian Bay was still as beautiful as ever. She would find Brad and ask him whether he'd like to go swimming. Twenty-four hours would soon pass, and she would prove to Adam that she was not as disillusioned as he imagined.

However, before she could put her plan into operation something else happened. She was still standing in the reception hall, waiting for Pam to find her son, when Corinne Leyton strolled through the swing doors. Today the other girl was wearing a purple thigh-length tee-shirt over white cotton trousers, her vivid hair confined beneath a silk scarf tied turban-wise around her head. As on the night of the barbecue, she managed to look startling, and the long curling lashes swept the reception area in mild disdain before alighting on Julie.

'What a coincidence!' she drawled, sauntering towards her. 'You're exactly the person I wanted to see.'

Corinne was exactly the person Julie *least* wanted to see, but she stood her ground and surveyed the other girl with what she hoped was equal composure.

'You wanted to see me?'

'Well, not me, actually, darling. Mommy. She asked me

151

to come over and invite you to Forest Bay for tea. You do take tea, don't you, Julie? All English people take tea.'

Julie expelled her breath on an uneasy sigh. 'It's very kind of your mother to invite me, but——'

'Oh, don't say no.' Corinne puckered her lips. 'Mommy will be so disappointed. She so much wants to get to know you. And I mean—if you're going to become part of the family ...'

Julie's face suffused with colour. She didn't believe for the smallest instant that Corinne really meant what she said. This was the girl who had expected to marry Dan, if all the portents were true. And whether or not he intended to marry her, she was hardly likely to offer the hand of friendship to a rival.

'I don't think having tea with your mother would be a good idea, Corinne,' she said now, refusing to address her as *Miss* Leyton. 'If you'd thank her for me, and——'

'Would you like her to come here?' suggested Corinne mildly. 'She will, you know, if you refuse. And somehow I don't think your friends would appreciate the gesture. I mean, Mommy can be a good friend—or a bad enemy.'

'Are you threatening me, Corinne?' Julie was appalled.

'No.' The girl shook her head, giving the student behind the reception desk a considering look as she did so. 'I'm only saying that Mommy is the wrong person to cross. Remember, the Galloways have to live here after you've gone.'

Julie bent her head. 'That's blackmail!'

'Oh, no!' Corinne uttered a light laugh. 'You English are so serious, aren't you? You take everything so personally. All you're being offered is an invitation to tea. Now that's not so bad, is it?'

Julie shook her head. 'I'm not so naïve, Corinne. Your mother wants to talk about Dan, doesn't she? About our love for one another. She thinks now that Dan's gone away ...'

'You know about that?' Corinne sounded surprised, and Julie stared at her.

'Of course I know. He rang me and told me, this morning.'

Corinne grimaced. 'Oh, well. I expect he had his reasons. But I wouldn't like to think any guy who professed love for me would take off for Miami without me.'

'For Miami?' echoed Julie disbelievingly, then pulled herself up. This was just another ploy, she thought incredulously. Now they were going to tell her that Dan hadn't gone to see his father at all. That having achieved his objective so far as she was concerned, he was now in pursuit of other amusement.

'Didn't you know?' Corinne asked now, arching those ridiculously dark brows. 'Mommy said that probably you wouldn't. But then she didn't know Dan had rung you. That was really something, wasn't it? I guess I have to give him full marks for initiative.'

'Will you go away, Corinne.' There was just so much that Julie could take, and right now she was coming to the end of her tether. 'I don't want to listen to any more of your lies, or your mother's lies either, for that matter. I believe Dan. I believe he loves me. And wherever he's gone and for whatever reason, he will come back. I know it.'

Corinne's lips twisted. 'You really cling, don't you, Julie? Dan said you would, but I didn't believe him. I mean, I'd die before I'd do what you're doing. You know he doesn't have any intention of marrying you, but still you hang on with those sharp little claws of yours. Go home! Go back to England where you belong. Go marry that smarmy lawyer of yours, and save yourself a lot of pain and humiliation!'

Julie turned away, almost stumbling as she went down the steps that gave access to the tree-shaded courtyard beyond. The air briefly revived her, but she hurried as she made her way to her cabin, pushing open the door and closing it behind her with hands that shook as she fumbled with the lock.

Then she flung herself on her bed, burying her face against the hand-worked coverlet, and letting the tears she had been suppressing since Dan's phone call give her the release she needed.

It was early evening before she lifted her head. The exhaustion of her tears had given way to sleep and she awakened from a heavy slumber feeling hollow-eyed and desperate.

Getting up, she sluiced her face under cold water and then surveyed her reflection in the mirror above the basin. She looked awful, she thought wearily, but then no one was going to care about that. All the same, she couldn't allow herself to remain in that state, and she spent time reapplying her make-up to hide the worst ravages of her grief.

Brushing her hair, she tried to think positively, but it was difficult when she knew so little of the facts. Dan had told her his father was ill. Adam said that the previous day Lionel Prescott had been speaking with his sister. She sighed. Dan had said he was going to New York. Corinne had said it was Miami, and while she didn't trust the other girl, she doubted she would tell an outright lie. And yet why not? If it was true, Dan had lied, and they were members of the same family.

Her head ached with the effort of trying to make some sense of what she ought to do. Dan had said stay, she kept telling herself, but what if he didn't come back? How long could she suffer Pam and David's sympathy? How long before humiliation forced her to pack her bags and leave?

Putting down the brush, she walked across to the windows, staring out disconsolately at the lengthening shadows. It was evening; it would soon be night. What kind of a creature was she if she couldn't give him the benefit of the doubt? He had said he would be back tomorrow or the day after. Until that time, she had to *believe* ...

She ate dinner alone, Adam apparently deciding to give her a breathing space, and then retired to her cabin early to watch television. But the constant interruption of the advertisements irritated her, and presently she turned the television off again and stared broodingly into the gathering dark.

Morning brought a respite from her tortuous thoughts. Brad joined her for breakfast, and with him she could briefly forget the problems that were troubling her.

'You want to go water-skiing, Julie?' he suggested hopefully, watching her with anxious eyes, and she hesitated only a moment before nodding her head.

'Water-skiing it is,' she agreed, her smile bringing animation to her pale features, and Brad whooped his delight to the restaurant in general.

Changing into her bikini in the cabin, Julie couldn't help but remember the last occasion she had put on a swimsuit. That day, the day she had spent with Dan, had assumed a state of unreality already, and she wondered if she had only imagined his tenderness and sensitivity.

Brad offered no such soul-searching. His was a simple companionship, an undemanding friendship, that had no hidden significance, that held no traumatic threat. Being with Brad was like being with a favourite younger brother, and she wondered how much different her life would have been if she had had a brother or a sister.

Her own attempts at water-skiing were no more successful than before, and she returned to the hotel at lunchtime exhausted by her efforts. Still, she had provided Brad with a lot of amusement, and they were laughing together as they climbed the steps to the hotel and found Adam waiting for them at the top.

'Ah, Julie,' he said, dismissing the boy with a patronising

gesture. 'I've been waiting for you. I have a message—from Forest Bay. I thought you should see it right away.'

'A message? From Dan?' Julie was instantly alarmed. 'What is it? Where is it? Let me see it!'

'It's here, it's here.' Adam was annoyingly unperturbed. He handed her the envelope calmly. 'It came just after you left. That chauffeur person brought it.'

'How do you know it's from Dan?' Julie exclaimed, tearing open the flap with frantic fingers, and Adam shrugged.

'I never said it was from Prescott,' he retorted mildly. 'I said it was from Forest Bay. Is it from him?'

Julie scanned the note she had extracted with anxious eyes, seeking the signature first. It was from Dan, and her heart flipped a beat as she turned back to the beginning. It was brief and to the point. He had written it before he left the previous day. It said simply that he was sorry he had lied to her, but he had not wanted to hurt her, and perhaps this letter would make it easier for her. He did care for her, but not deeply enough to oppose his parents' wishes, and while she might imagine they could make a good life for themselves, he knew it would never work. He knew if he had tried to tell her she would have tried to persuade him otherwise, and there was no point in continuing a relationship that had never been intended as a lasting one.

Julie swayed a little as the last words swam before her eyes. Words of love and affection, and of his hope that she would be happy with Adam if she chose to marry him. She felt sick and empty, and totally devastated, and she just wished she could crawl into some corner and die.

'Is it bad news?'

Adam was looking at her strangely, and she didn't like the avidity in his expression. It was as if he knew exactly what was in the letter, and she was loathe to tell him and satisfy that speculative gleam. She bent her head, crushing the parchment between her fingers, and then looked up to find his eyes were unexpectedly gentle.

'You don't have to tell me, you know,' he said quietly. 'I can always tell what you're thinking. Come away with me, Julie. Leave this place. Let's go now—this afternoon. Before anything else happens.'

'What else can happen?' asked Julie dully, looking down at the envelope in her hands. 'But—all right, Adam, I will go away with you.' *Anything to escape!* 'Just leave me alone now. I—I need to think.'

'Of course.' With a brief smile he turned away, and she watched him stride firmly across the square. Beside the broader Canadians he seemed thin, slight—and older than she could remember.

Her own passage to her cabin was less confident. Once there, she sank down on the bed and re-read the note, noticing inconsequently what an unusual hand Dan had. She would have expected his writing to be like him, firm and aggressive. Instead it was almost tentative, the ts and ls looped with a feminine attention to detail. Something else she realised, too. Once again she had only Adam's word that the note was from Dan. She had never seen his handwriting, so how could she be sure this was it?

Her head began to throb. Surely, surely Anthea Leyton would not sink to this! Was this why she had asked to see her the previous afternoon? Had she devised this letter—this very carefully written letter? How could she find out? There was no way.

Getting up from the bed again, she stared at her reflection in the mirror. Was she a fool to suspect anything? Was the letter genuine? Was she clutching at straws in this attempt to hold on to her beliefs? Or was she, as Corinne had said, clinging to a dream, a state of unreality, becoming one of those girls that his aunt had deplored to Pam and David?

She didn't know what to do, who to turn to. Pam could tell her nothing, nor could David. They would probably accept the letter at its face value. Obviously Adam would. It confirmed everything he had said.

Shaking her head, she picked up the envelope and smoothed it out, and as she did so she saw something she had not noticed before. The envelope was not addressed to her, not to her personally, that was. It was addressed to the Kawana Point Hotel, just as the invitation had been three days ago.

Blinking, she stared at it in disbelief. Were she to give in to her vivid imagination once again she would say that it was the *same* envelope. But it couldn't be. If that were so ... *if that were so*, it would mean someone here had written the letter, someone at the hotel ...

With her breathing quickening in concert with her agitation, she examined the handwriting once again. It wasn't like Adam's handwriting, but then, if it was he who had written the letter, obviously he would have disguised it. And perhaps that was why it looked so detailed, why the loops were so carefully drawn. Had someone invented the style just for the purposes of disguise?

She sank down again weakly. Would Adam do such a thing? she asked herself half impatiently. He was upset with her, that was true, but inventing a letter like this ... It didn't make sense. He must know that sooner or later he would be found out. All the same, it did occur to her that they could well be married by that time. He had already suggested getting married in the United States, travelling around, moving from place to place. It could be weeks before any communication from Dan reached them ...

Trembling now, as much from inner cold as an outer one, she went quickly into the bathroom and took a shower. Then, without giving herself time to think or change her mind, she dressed in the fringed suede suit she had worn to travel in, collected her bag and passport, and left the cabin.

David's motor launch was waiting at the jetty, and she

was glad she knew how to handle it. The engine fired at the second attempt, and with slightly unsteady fingers she steered it out of the marina and across the expanse of blue water towards the dock at Midland.

She spent a frustrating twelve hours trying to get to New York. She had no visa, and she was forced to spend a long time at the United States Consulate in Toronto to get one. This took valuable time, but at least she was able to fly direct from there to New York, and she arrived at Kennedy airport very late in the evening.

The time that had elapsed since those moments in the cabin when she had conceived the idea of coming to New York and confronting Dan herself had had a debilitating effect on her nerves, and sitting in the airport building, waiting for a cab to take her into the city, she felt isolated from everything—and everyone—she had ever known and loved. It was as if she was in limbo, between the world she knew and the world she didn't, and indeed the world which might not want to know her.

Because she knew the names of few hotels in New York, she asked the driver to take her to the Pierre, then sat back enthralled to watch the encroaching lights of the city. In spite of her anxiety, it was impossible not to be thrilled at this her first sight of that most famous of skylines, and she gazed through the car window in fascination as they crossed the Triborough bridge and ploughed through the suburbs of Manhattan.

The Pierre stood at the junction of Fifth Avenue and Sixty-First Street, and Julie was soon standing at the window of her allotted room looking out on the sleeping city. Only it didn't appear to be sleeping, she thought wryly, hearing the curious whooping of a police car from beyond the tree-shrouded mass of Central Park.

Still, she had to have some sleep, she thought, before facing whatever ordeal was to come, and after washing her face and brushing her teeth, she sank wearily into the comfortable bed.

She must have slept, because when she opened her eyes the room was bright and sunlit, and from below her windows there was the increasing hum of the traffic.

She rang room service and ordered toast and coffee, then took another shower before putting on the suede suit once more. At least the slim skirt was not creased, she saw with relief, and by the time her tray was delivered she had examined the telephone directory and discovered, to her dismay, exactly how many Prescotts there were in the inner city area.

Drinking black coffee, she decided gloomily that she would have to ring the bank. Whether or not they would be prepared to give her Dan's address was another matter, but at least she had to try. Other than that, she could only visualise making calls to every Prescott listed in the book.

The main branch of the Scott National Bank appeared to be on Sixth Avenue, the Avenue of the Americas, and she dialled their number first, waiting impatiently for them to answer. But there was no reply, and glancing at her watch, she realised why. It was only a little after nine o'clock, and the bank wouldn't even be open yet.

Finishing her breakfast, she left the hotel and walked restlessly along Fifth Avenue, looking in shop windows. The layout of the city was in squares, or blocks, and the numbering of the streets and avenues made it a simple matter to work out how far it was to any particular junction. She understood now why Americans denoted distance in blocks. The city was built like a gigantic crossword puzzle.

Despite what she had heard, she was not accosted on her walk, and she was pleasantly surprised by the cleanliness of the city. She liked the banks of fountains, too, that provided the constant sound of running water, and the sometimes crazy antics of the cabs, that each possessed the inevitable ravages of constant competition.

It was after ten-thirty by the time she returned to the Pierre, and the doorman greeted her politely. 'Did you enjoy your walk, ma'am?' he enquired, opening the door for her, and she thanked him as she assured him that she had enjoyed it very much.

This time a receptionist responded to her call to the bank, but when she asked whether it was possible for them to give her Mr Daniel Prescott's address, there was a flurry of activity.

'Mr Daniel Prescott, Miss Osbourne?' the girl asked after ascertaining her name, and Julie said: 'That's right,' in faintly breathless tones.

The line went dead for a while after that, and she suspected she had been disconnected. After all, she could be anyone calling to ask for Dan's address, but she continued to hold on and hope for the best.

Eventually another female voice came on the line:

'Miss Osbourne?'

'Yes.' Julie swallowed with difficulty. 'Who am I speaking to, please?'

'I'm Mara Elliot, Miss Osbourne. Mr *Lionel* Prescott's secretary. Would I be right in thinking you are a Miss *Julie* Osbourne?'

Her voice had definitely Southern overtones, but Julie was hardly in a state to register anything. 'I—why, yes,' she got out chokingly. 'Do—do you know about me?'

'Mr Prescott isn't here right now,' Mara Elliot continued, without answering her question, 'but I know he'd surely like to meet you, Miss Osbourne. So if you could come by at say—twelve-thirty, I could try to arrange for you to see him then.'

Julie licked her dry lips. 'To—to see *Dan*?'

'No, Miss Osbourne. For you to meet Mr Lionel Prescott, Dan's father.'

Julie was stunned, as much by the realisation that this girl seemed to think Lionel Prescott would want to meet her as by the knowledge that Dan had been lying to her.

'I—er—I thought Mr Prescott was—was unwell,' she got out unevenly.

'Not to my knowledge,' Mara Elliot denied smoothly. 'Will twelve-thirty be all right with you?'

'Twelve-thirty? Oh—no, no.' Julie couldn't even think straight. 'That is, it doesn't matter, thank you. I've made a mistake. I'm sorry I troubled you——'

'Wait!' the other girl sensed she was about to ring off and interrupted her. 'If—if I could get in touch with Dan——'

'That won't be necessary.' Julie's words were clipped and tense. 'Thank you for your assistance.'

'And if Dan comes into the office? Where shall I tell him he can get in touch with you?'

'He can't,' said Julie tightly. 'G'bye.'

Of course she cried again, more bitterly now, but sufficiently energetically to obliterate her make-up and leave her eyes all red and puffy. She was a mess, she thought miserably, surveying herself in the mirror above the chest of drawers. She *was* a mess and she had *made* a mess of her life. Were the Osbournes fated never to find happiness?

She didn't feel like any lunch, so she remained in her room, lying on her bed, trying to plan what she should do now. The letter had faded into insignificance beside these latest revelations, but if Adam had written it, he had destroyed the last links between them.

She must have dozed because she awakened with a start to the phone's ringing. She was slightly dazed, but she couldn't imagine who might be ringing her here, and guessing it must be the manager, she groped for the receiver.

'Miss Osbourne?' It was the receptionist. 'We have a visitor for you, waiting in the hall. Would you like me to send him up?'

'*Him?*' Julie swallowed convulsively. 'Who—who is it?'

'A Mr Prescott, ma'am.'

'Oh!' Dan? Julie blinked rapidly. 'Oh, no! That is—ask him to wait. I—I'll come down.'

How had he found her?

Scrambling off the bed, she stared in agony at her reflection. Pale cheeks, hollow eyes, traces of puffiness around the lids—how could she face him like this? And why had he come here? What could he possibly have to say to her now?

With trembling fingers she rinsed her face and then applied her make-up. Blusher only made her look hectic, like a painted doll, so she had to be content with looking pale, though hardly interesting, she thought unhappily. At least her hair was soft and silky, and if she brushed it forward it tended to distract attention from her sallow features.

The suede suit would have to do, she had no alternative, and picking up her handbag, she gave herself one last dissatisfied appraisal before walking the carpeted corridor to the elevator.

Downstairs in the lobby she looked about her anxiously, wanting to be prepared for this meeting. She didn't want him to come upon her unannounced, and she hurried across to the reception desk to find out where he was waiting.

'In here, ma'am,' the young man behind the desk directed smilingly, and Julie stepped hesitantly into the discreetly-lit atmosphere of the bar.

It took her a moment to adjust her eyes, but before she could assimilate her surroundings a light hand touched her arm and an unfamiliar male voice said: 'Julie?'

She looked up, startled, into eyes she recognised in a face she didn't. And yet the similarity was there, the way his hair grew back from his temples, although in this case it was liberally streaked with grey, and the faintly sensual curve of his mouth. It had to be Dan's father, and she panicked.

'I—*no*,' she said foolishly, realising her accent was giving her away, and then heaved a heavy sigh. 'That is, I am Julie, yes, but I didn't—want—*expect* to see you, Mr Prescott.'

'That's good,' he said mildly. 'You know who I am. Now shall we stop all this jittering and sit down?'

'Oh, but I——'

Julie glanced back longingly over her shoulder, then realising there was no escape, she acquiesced. Lionel Prescott saw her comfortably ensconced on the banquette, and ordered two Martinis before seating himself beside her. Then, when their drinks were set before them, he gave her a slightly rueful smile.

'So,' he said. 'At last we get to meet.'

'How did you find me?'

The words were out before she could stop them, but Lionel Prescott didn't seem to mind.

'Well, I could say I hired a gang of private eyes to do the work for me,' he remarked dryly, 'but I don't want to worsen the impression you probably have of me, so I'll admit that Dan told me.'

'*Dan told you?*'

'That's right. He got the information from the Consulate in Toronto, would you believe?'

Julie blinked, and then she remembered that when she applied for her visa she had had to state where she intended to stay in New York. But if Dan had found that out, it must mean he had returned to Georgian Bay ...

CHAPTER ELEVEN

SHE was staring blankly into space when Lionel Prescott spoke again. 'It doesn't really matter how I found you. The fact is, I have, and I can't deny I'm relieved. My son means everything to me, and while I may have many faults, interfering with his life is not one of them.'

Julie's brows descended and she turned to stare at him in disbelief. 'You mean—you mean Dan has—has told you—about—about us?'

'You didn't know?'

Julie shook her head. 'I—I didn't know what to think.'

'But I understood him to tell me that——'

'He said you were ill, Mr Prescott,' Julie broke in defensively. 'And you're not, are you?'

'Ah ...' Lionel Prescott nodded slowly. 'You found out about that. Who told you? Anthea? Corinne? Dan guessed the minute he was out of sight they'd try to interfere.'

'Then why didn't he warn me?' exclaimed Julie half tearfully, not fully recovered from the emotive upheaval she had suffered. 'And—and why didn't he tell me the truth?'

Lionel sighed. 'That was my fault, I'm afraid. I asked him not to.'

Julie couldn't take this in, and with a sympathetic shrug Lionel added: 'This isn't really the place to discuss such things, but it will have to do. I asked Dan to come and see me because of a message I'd received.'

'A message?' Julie stared at him.

'From a Mr Price?'

'Adam?'

'I guess that is his name.'

Julie put a hand to her head. 'But—but why would Adam

send a message to you? What could he possibly have to tell you?'

'Can't you guess?'

Julie's throat closed up. 'Oh, God!' Then she shook her head. 'But I told Dan!'

'I know it.'

'But why would Adam do such a thing?'

'I imagine because he thought it might influence us against you.'

Julie hesitated. 'And—and that was why you sent for Dan?'

'Partly.'

'Then I'm afraid I don't understand. Where is Dan? Why are you here? What are you trying to tell me?'

'Be patient,' he advised gently. 'At this moment in time,' he consulted the gold watch around his wrist, 'Dan ought to be in the airplane bound for Kennedy. He'll be here in a couple of hours. And I'm here to prevent you running out on him again.'

Julie was confused. 'You knew I called your office?'

'Or course. Mara rang me at once, and as I'd already had Dan on the phone from Forest Bay explaining that you'd disappeared ...' He grimaced. 'We were all very relieved, believe me.'

Julie shook her head. 'If Dan had only explained ...'

'What about? Price's message? Or the publicity his actions are likely to promote?'

'Whose actions? What publicity?' Julie was bewildered. 'Mr Prescott, if there's something more to this, something I should know ...'

'I don't think it's my place, Julie,' he said quietly, and she gazed at him in bafflement. And then, as if responding to her evident consternation, he added: 'You'll find out soon enough, I guess.'

'Mr Prescott, please ...' Julie was almost beside herself. 'Has this to do with Dan and me? Did he tell you he'd asked me to marry him?'

'He did.' Lionel Prescott nodded.

'And—and you don't—disapprove?'

'Julie!' He took one of her hands in both of his. 'Dan has his own life to lead. You want me to be honest with you? All right, I'll tell you. His mother and I, we did hope he would marry a nice American girl. But I didn't, so why should I expect him to?'

Julie shook her head. 'Your sister—Corinne——'

'I know, I know. But although I have three daughters, I have only one son, Julie, and I don't intend to lose him. And I know I would if I tried to stand in his way. He's a pretty easy-going guy normally, but then so am I. However, if you cross him ...' He shrugged. 'You know what I mean?'

Julie nodded, rather tremulously. 'I know.'

'So that's cleared that up. I'm not saying Dan's mother's going to greet you with open arms—that's not her way. But she respects Dan's wishes, and you know—I think she just might admire your spirit.'

Julie pressed her lips together. 'So—so if it's not to do with Dan and me, why did you mention Adam—and publicity?'

Lionel sighed. 'Julie——'

'It concerns me, doesn't it? Don't I have a right to know?'

'A right to know?' echoed Dan's father reflectively. 'Yes, I guess you do at that. But Julie, these things are better handled by lawyers, you know. I'm just a banker. I wouldn't know how to tell you.'

'Then just say it,' she exclaimed. 'Is it about—Daddy? He—he wasn't murdered or anything, was he?'

'No.' Lionel pressed her hand once more and released it. 'No, I'm afraid your father took his own life. However, I can tell you it has to do with—why he died.'

Julie stared at him. 'Did Adam have something to do

with that?' She shook her head. 'But they were friends! And in any case, how could you find out a thing like that?'

Lionel studied her pale cheeks for several seconds, then he seemed to come to a decision. 'All right,' he said. 'I'll explain what happened, at least so far as I am concerned.' He paused. 'I told you I had a message from Price, didn't I? It was—let me see—four days ago now. The day you and Dan spent on the yacht, is that right?' Julie nodded, and he went on: 'I got this telephone message, relayed via Anthea, to the effect that—well, that I ought to be warned there was instability in your family.'

'I see.'

Lionel frowned. 'Up until then, I hardly knew of your existence. Dan's mother and I have been in Miami for the past three weeks——'

Miami!

'—and although Anthea had phoned a couple of times complaining that Dan was getting mixed up with some English girl, we hadn't taken her seriously.'

Julie quivered. She could still scarcely believe that Dan was serious!

'Anyway, your father's name was familiar to me, and really almost—accidentally, I learned of Price's involvement.'

'He was my father's partner.'

'Yes, my dear, I know.' Lionel looked solemn. 'Exactly how well do you know him?'

'Very well. I've known him since I was tiny. And—and after my mother died and Daddy became—sort of withdrawn, he used to try to take his place.'

'Mmm.' Lionel sounded doubtful. 'Your father was in debt, I gather.'

'That's right. Only Adam's money saved the firm from bankruptcy.'

'Is that so?' Again there was a pregnant pause. 'How do you know all this?'

'Adam told me. After Daddy was dead. He—he had got into difficulties with interest payments. There was a considerable sum of money involved. Several thousand pounds, I think. He couldn't face prison, so he took his own life.'

Lionel was watching her closely now as he said: 'Just how did taking his own life solve anything?'

'Oh ...' Julie shrugged. 'There was insurance. Adam dealt with all that. He said Daddy had done the only thing left to him, in the circumstances.'

'I see.' Lioned sighed. 'And you never questioned that?'

'Questioned it? No. Why should I?' Julie was puzzled.

'Julie, insurance companies don't pay out in cases of suicide.'

'Oh, I know that, but Adam said this was a special case.'

'A special case?'

'Yes.'

'Julie, there is no such thing as a special case. Not where suicide is concerned. Can you imagine? Every guy who got into financial difficulties and thought of suicide would insure himself several times over. It's just not on, honey. Insurance companies are not benevolent societies. Believe me, I know!'

Julie stared at him. 'But if there was no insurance money ...'

'Exactly. Where did the money come from?'

'Yes.'

'Would you believe Price?'

'Adam?' Julie blinked: 'But if he could do that ...'

'—why didn't he do it sooner?'

She swallowed. 'Yes.'

Lionel sighed. 'I don't know how to tell you this, honey, but the way I hear it, Price had bought up all your father's debts long before the crash came.'

'No!'

'That's the way it's looking.'

'But how do you know all this?'

Lionel hesitated. 'I have friends. Friends in England. Relatives, moreover. I made a couple of phone calls, that's all.'

'After—Adam contacted you?'

'That's right.' He shrugged. 'I'll admit, I wanted to know more about this girl that Dan was getting involved with.'

Julie shook her head. 'But what did you mean about publicity?' She moved her shoulders helplessly. 'How did anyone get to know?'

'These things invariably come out, Julie. I suspect that Price got careless when he thought he'd gotten away with it. Whatever, it must suit his purpose to be out of England right now.'

Julie tried to make sense of her thoughts. It was true, Adam had been unusually willing to leave his beloved apartment and come to Canada, and he had deterred her from going home. But could it be true? Could he have professed friendship for her father and stabbed him in the back like that? It didn't make sense. They had been partners for so long ...

'But why?' she murmured now, hardly aware she was voicing her thoughts aloud, and Lionel said softly:

'Perhaps you were the catalyst. Have you thought of that?'

'*Me?*'

'Yes, you. Didn't Dan tell me that Price wanted to marry you?'

'Well, yes. But Daddy knew all about that.'

'Did he approve?'

Julie hesitated. 'I—I think so.'

'Didn't he think the man was too old for you? Dan says he's at least seventeen years your senior.'

'Well, he is, I know, but——' Julie broke off helplessly. 'It was just taken for granted.'

'By Price?'

'And—and me,' she admitted, unable to absolve herself of all blame.

Lionel reached for his Martini. 'Oh, well, maybe we'll never know the truth. The fact remains, he seems a pretty contemptible guy. Don't you think so?'

Julie said nothing. She couldn't. She was too shocked to make any judgment. But one thing more needed to be confirmed. Opening her handbag, she extracted the letter she had stuffed there the previous morning and handed it to him.

'I—I received this,' she said jerkily, realising now that Dan could have had nothing to do with it.

Lionel studied the letter disbelievingly. 'My God! You don't imagine Dan wrote this, do you?'

Julie licked her dry lips. 'I didn't know what to think at first. He'd signed it. I couldn't tell whether it was his handwriting or not ...'

Lionel nodded. 'It's not, I can tell you that.' He paused. 'And if it had been writen at Forest Bay, the notepaper would have been identifiable. Anthea has everything monogrammed.' He frowned as he examined the envelope. 'This is monogrammed!'

'I know.' Julie heaved a sigh. 'I think it's the envelope our invitation to your sister's barbecue came in.'

Lionel turned it over in his hands. 'So you're suggesting someone else wrote this letter. Who? Price?'

Julie shrugged. 'Perhaps.'

'Is this why you came to New York?'

She nodded again. 'I had to know, one way or the other. I had to speak to Dan. But when I discovered you hadn't been ill——'

'You thought the worst?'

'Yes.'

'Oh, Julie!' He touched her cheek with a gentle hand. 'You've had a hard time. And it's all been my fault. I told

Dan to make that excuse. I wanted to warn him about Price, and I didn't know what your reaction might be. I had to speak with Dan alone.'

Julie felt too dazed to think coherently. So much had happened in such a short space of time, she couldn't absorb it all, and all that was real was that Dan loved her and wanted her, and she could believe in him.

Towards Adam she felt an intense feeling of incredulity. Even now, without Lionel Prescott's words ringing in her ears, she could hardly accept what she had learned. And yet she had the evidence in her own hands. The letter—which he had delivered so callously—he must have banked on her lack of confidence in herself to swing the balance. And it almost had, let's face it, she thought deploringly. Without the strength of her love for Dan, she might well have taken the easy way out, and once she and Adam had left Georgian Bay it would have been incredibly difficult to find them.

She shivered a little in the wake of this conclusion. Everything could have gone so badly wrong for her, just as it had for her father, and thinking of those debts William Osbourne had run up, she realised the torment he must have gone through. She tried to recall whether he had shown any opposition to Adam's plans, but all that she remembered was his indifference towards her, which she had attributed to his grief after her mother's death.

Noticing her drawn features, Lionel exclaimed: 'I wish I'd insisted that I should take you home with me, Julie, but as Dan said, I guess you two young people need to be alone together.' He sighed. 'I know, what say we take a ride down to the Prescott building? We've got plenty of time,' he smiled, 'and we can always leave Dan a message. A genuine one this time.'

Julie agreed. She needed the break from her own thoughts, and they rode the Avenue of the Americas to the giant skyscraper where the Prescott group of companies had their offices. The offices were closing, but walking the plate-glass walled halls and riding in along the high-speed elevators, Julie gained a little impression of the efficiency which had made the Prescott name so famous.

'You know what Mark Twain said, don't you?' Lionel remarked, as she surveyed the sumptuous appointments of his huge office, and when she shook her head, he went on: 'He said "In Boston they ask, how much does he know? In New York, how much is he worth?"' He grinned. 'I guess this place appals you, doesn't it?'

Julie made an awkward gesture. 'Not exactly——'

'But you don't find it impressive?'

'Mr Prescott, I realise you expected Dan to marry a rich girl——'

'I expected him to show good judgment, and you know something? I think he has.'

She stared at him. 'Were you testing me, Mr Prescott?'

He shrugged. 'I admit, I was curious to see how you would react to this place.'

'And if I'd reacted differently?'

'But you didn't,' said Lionel, tucking his hand under her elbow. 'And I'll be smug and say that I knew it all along. After all, I taught Dan everything he knows.'

Not everything, thought Julie dryly, but she didn't contradict him.

Back at the hotel, Julie entered the lobby half apprehensively. She was tired, more tired than she had realised, and she had yet to learn whether Dan had forgiven her. His father had been kind, but was she not expecting too much of their relationship? Had the time and the place not distorted their real feelings for one another?

She crossed the carpeted hall on leaden feet, and then saw Dan himself, standing beside the display cabinets, impatiently contemplating their contents. It was a different Dan, and yet the same, his casual clothes having given way to a dark grey business suit, the usual open-necked shirts replaced by a pristine white one, a dark tie slotted neatly beneath the collar. It accentuated his tan, and his hands pushed carelessly into the pockets of his pants drew her attention to the muscular length of his legs. Oh, God, she thought helplessly, I do love him, I *do*, and then faltered in mid-step as he turned and saw her.

'Julie . . .'

The word was uttered half under his breath, but she read her name on his lips as he strode eagerly towards her. Ignoring everyone, including his father behind her, he pulled her almost roughly into his arms, and his mouth on hers erased all the horrors of the last three days.

The kiss was not long, but it was hard and passionate, and their intimacy was in no doubt when he lifted his head. 'I've been nearly out of my mind,' he told her with barely suppressed anguish, and she touched his face almost wonderingly as she said:

'So have I.'

His eyes narrowed, returning to the parted sweetness of her mouth, and then realising they could not continue this conversation satisfactorily here, he forced himself to look beyond her to where his father was assuming a feigned interest in an enormous bowl of flowers occupying a central plinth.

'So you made it,' he said, addressing the older man, and Julie turned half tremulously to face her future father-in-law.

'Don't I always?' Lionel enquired dryly, giving Julie a conspiratorial smile, and Dan's hand on her shoulder tightened.

'Where were you?' he demanded. 'I've been waiting almost twenty minutes.'

'Didn't you get the message?' asked Lionel, frowning, and Dan nodded.

'Yeah, I got it,' he agreed, drawing Julie back against him, as if he couldn't bear for them to be apart. 'But what took you so long?'

'I was just showing your—Julie—your grandfather's office.'

'Oh,' Dan nodded, 'I get it. To see if she was impressed, right?'

Lionel shrugged. 'Julie and I—understand one another, I think.' He smiled again. 'You don't begrudge me that, do you?'

Dan looked down at Julie with lazily mocking eyes. 'I guess not,' he admitted. 'Just so long as you don't expect me to invite you to join us for dinner. We have a lot to say to one another.'

'My dismissal,' remarked Lionel wryly, grimacing at Julie once again. 'You'll come over to the house later?'

'Tomorrow,' said Dan firmly, and Julie quivered. 'Tell Ma not to worry. We won't elope. I promised her a proper wedding, and that's what she shall have. And you can tell her that she can arrange it, hmm?' This as he looked down at Julie. 'We're your family from now on,' he added huskily. 'And we want to do it right, don't we?'

Julie nodded, too full of emotion for speech, and Lionel decided the time had come to make his departure. 'Tomorrow, then,' he said, and after a moment's hesitation he leant forward and touched Julie's cheeks with his lips. 'We'll look forward to that,' he said gently, and left them.

With his father's departure, Dan swung her round to face him again, his face a little strained in the artificial lights of the lobby. 'Do you have a suite?' he demanded, and in breathless tones she explained she had a *room*. 'Okay,' he said. 'Let's go there, shall we?'

The look in his eyes was unguarded, and her lips parted in nervous anticipation. Nodding her head, she led the way along to the lifts, and suffered the bell-boy's cheerful patter as they ascended to the fourteenth floor.

Walking along the corridor, Dan didn't touch her, and she fumbled in her handbag for her key, pulling it out and dropping it, and having him retrieve it for her as they reached the panelled door. Dan himself opened the door, lifting the plastic card from inside and hanging it outside with the words *Do Not Disturb* plainly in view. Then he closed the door and attached the safety chain before reaching for her.

'Julie,' he groaned, pressing her body closely against him. 'Oh, Julie, don't ever do anything like that to me again!'

'I won't,' she whispered huskily, then wound her arms around his neck as his mouth searched for hers.

There was a hungry eagerness in his kiss, a kind of feverish desperation, born of the agonies of anxiety he had suffered in those hours before he knew where she had gone. It was as if he couldn't get enough of her, and her lips parted beneath his.

After the emotional torment she had gone through, it was infinitely satisfying having him holding her again, and she arched closer, uncaring in those moments that there were still so many things to be said between them, so many things to explain. She wanted him and she knew he wanted her, and no other assuagement would ease the aching hunger inside her.

Yet she found she was still nervous when he drew her to the bed, and touching the fine mohair of his jacket, she murmured: 'Your—your suit—you'll ruin it!'

His reaction was immediate. 'If you're worried, I'll take it off,' he said softly, unfastening his waistcoat, and suddenly her fears deserted her.

'Let me,' she breathed, brushing his fingers aside, and he offered no resistance as she unbuttoned his shirt and loosened his tie.

'Do you know what kind of a night I had last night?' he demanded at last, pressing her down on to the bed and covering her trembling body with his own. 'I was desperate, not knowing where you'd gone or what might have happened to you. And if I'd known you were here—in New York——'

'Don't talk,' said Julie huskily, winding her arms around his neck and pulling his mouth down to hers. 'Not now . . .'

Their lovemaking was as ardent and tumultuous as Julie remembered. Dan brought her every nerve and sinew alive, so that she wanted to join herself to him and never let him go. Looking up into his taut features as he brought her to the heights, sharing his release when it came, sliding down through the aeons of pleasure and ecstasy, she felt an enormous overflowing of love inside her, a deep sense of belonging, of involvement, of feeling herself a part of this man just as he was a part of her.

'No one—but no one—has ever made me feel as you do,' he groaned at last, lifting his face from the moist hollow of her nape. 'Oh, Julie, I love you so much. How could you believe I'd walk out on you?'

'You told me your father was sick,' she reminded him huskily, sliding possessive fingers along his thigh, and he sought her mouth once more before answering her.

'Didn't he explain that?' he asked, against her lips, and she moved her head in silent acknowledgement. 'He wanted to tell me about Price.'

'I know.' Julie shifted sensuously beneath him. 'But that wasn't all.'

'What else could there be?' Dan protested, imprisoning her teasing fingers. 'Julie, be still. What do you mean—that isn't all?'

Julie sighed. 'Let me get up and I'll show you.'

Dan pulled a wry face. 'Is that absolutely necessary?'

'Only if you want to know.'

Dan drew an unsteady breath. 'I don't want to let you go.'

'Then don't,' she whispered, her tongue appearing in silent provocation, and for a while there was only the sound of their tormented breathing in the room.

It was much later when Dan eventually rolled on to his

back, letting her get off the bed. His eyes followed her, however, and half provocatively she put on his shirt, rolling up the sleeves and wrapping its folds closely about her. Then she picked up her handbag and took out the letter she had shown Lionel Prescott earlier.

'Here,' she said huskily. 'Now perhaps you'll understand.'

Dan sat up, pushing back his hair with a lazy hand. He frowned as he unfolded the letter, but the frown had deepened into a scowl when he had read it.

'The swine!' he muttered, crumpling it into a ball. 'The swine! So that was what he meant!'

Julie came to perch on the end of the bed, long legs curled under her. 'What who meant? Adam?'

'Yes, *Adam*!' said Dan savagely. 'The creep! I'd like to twist his guts!'

Julie shook her head. 'You've spoken to him?'

'Of course. Didn't my father tell you?'

'No. He—he only said what—what he had told you.'

Dan nodded, massaging the back of his neck with both hands. 'I guess he thought it would be easier if I told you. But—*hell*, it's not.' He looked at her compassionately. 'Honey, can't we just forget it?'

'Forget what?'

'Price! And his involvement with us! I doubt you'll ever see him again.'

'You mean—he's gone?'

Dan nodded. 'He took off right after our little—altercation. Don't ask me where. I don't want to know.'

Julie stretched out a hand and touched his knee, her fingers warm and gentle. 'Dan ...' She gazed at him adoringly. 'If it's to do with my father, can't you tell me? Let's start as we mean to go on. Don't let's have any secrets from one another.'

'It's not my secret!' he muttered harshly, capturing her hand and carrying it to his lips. 'But maybe you're right.

Maybe Price will always stand between us if you don't know the truth.'

Julie nodded, and with a sigh he went on: 'Exactly what did Dad tell you? I guess you don't know about—about your father's debts, do you?'

'Yes,' Julie reassured him. 'Your father didn't want to tell me, but I persuaded him.'

'Ah!' Dan breathed a sigh of relief, pressing his lips to her palm before continuing. 'Okay, so you know that Price had been running the business for a number of years.'

'I suppose he had.' This was something Julie had not thought of.

Dan nodded. 'What I guess you don't know is why—why your father killed himself.'

'Because of the debts!'

Dan shook his head. 'I thought that at first. But it didn't altogether make sense. I mean, he'd been in debt for years. Why should it suddenly become too much for him?'

Julie frowned. 'And you know why?'

'I didn't. I was still puzzling that one out when Price himself supplied the answer.'

'Adam?'

Dan sighed. 'Julie, I was desperate. You'd disappeared, and no one knew where you'd gone. I didn't even know why you'd taken off like that, and nor did the Galloways. They knew nothing about this letter, did they? Only two people knew about it. You—and the person who wrote it.'

'Adam.'

'Everything comes down to him, doesn't it?' Dan pressed her cool fingers against his hot forehead. 'Okay—so I went to find Price. He was in your cabin. He seemed to be looking for something. I guess now it was the letter. He looked pretty sick when he saw me.'

'You told him you knew about——'

'Sure. I guess I said some pretty disgusting things, but whatever, it got him riled, the way I wanted him to be riled. A man can make mistakes when he's angry he'd never make when he's not. I told him that whatever happened, I intended *you* should know the truth before you entered into any further contract with him, and I think it dawned on him you weren't about to come back. Not to him, anyway.'

Julie stared at him. 'He didn't mention the letter?'

'Not in so many words. He only said that after what had happened, you'd never want to see me again, but I didn't know what he meant by that. And in any case, I was too hell-bent to care too much over the subtleties. I just wanted him to know that the English press were getting mightily interested in his affairs, and a police investigation was on the cards. I guess that threw him. Anyway, he went on about you—how he'd done it all for you——'

'For me!'

'—and how your father had defrauded him.'

'Daddy?'

Dan nodded, holding her startled eyes with his own. 'Yes. Apparently Price lent your father the money as a kind of—down-payment. For you!'

'Oh, Dan!'

He shook his head. 'I'm sorry, honey, but it's true. Your father was never for the deal, and I guess he tried every way to get out of it.'

'And when he couldn't ...'

Dan pressed her fingers to his lips. 'Don't blame yourself, sweetheart. You couldn't help it. Price was relentless. I guess he knew you'd be finished school in a couple of months. Maybe he gave your father an ultimatum. Whatever, he couldn't take it.'

'If only he'd told me!'

'I guess he knew that if he did——'

'—I'd insist on marrying Adam?' Julie bent her head. 'He knew I would.'

Dan tugged her gently towards him. 'So Price lost his

gamble. He saved your father's name at the expense of his own.'

'Oh, Dan!'

He sighed, pulling her close against him. 'Listen: your father could have gone to prison——'

'He knew I'd never allow that.'

'—so he did the only thing possible.'

'But I could still have married Adam,' she exclaimed, half tearfully, and he cradled her head against his shoulder.

'There is one more thing,' he told her gently. 'He did confide in someone.'

'Who?' Julie lifted her head to stare at him.

'A—Mrs Collins?'

'Our housekeeper?'

Dan nodded. 'I don't know how much he told her. Maybe just that he was worried about your relationship with Price.'

'But she never said a word to me!'

'Perhaps when you went away she didn't realise how serious it was.' He paused. 'But from what my father learned from London, I would say that Price has been making a nuisance of himself, going to the house, acting as if he owned it already. It got her thinking—and talking.'

'And that's how the story came out?'

'Honey, where suicide is concerned, particularly in the case of someone like your father, the press is always interested.'

'I can't believe it!'

'What? about Price?'

'No. That—that Daddy would agree to such a thing.'

'He was desperate, too, remember? And your mother was very ill, wasn't she?'

Julie nodded. 'She fell, quite by accident, and injured her spine. The condition developed complications, a spinal infection that affected her brain——'

'Don't go on,' said Dan huskily. 'I know all about it. Do you remember when you told me your father had committed suicide?'

'On the wharf? I remember.'

'Yes. Well, I had Uncle Maxwell find out all the facts for me then. I wanted to know everything about you.'

'And—and it didn't—deter you?'

'Does it look like it?' he murmured dryly, his lips against her temple. 'Price knew that, too. I guess he decided to get out while he could.'

'Where has he gone?'

'I don't know. Maybe the police will catch up with him. Whatever happens, nothing can bring your father back.'

'No.'

Julie nodded, and with an effort Dan said : 'How would you like to get dressed now and go out for dinner?'

'Is that what you want?'

'Me?' Dan's grin was rueful. 'No. But it's what you want to do that matters. Tomorrow you'll be meeting my mother. That's my decision. Tonight is yours.'

'Then let's eat up here,' said Julie throatily. 'We can ring room service, and——'

'You're delicious, do you know that?' he exclaimed, pulling her down on top of him. 'You can read my mind. Going out and sharing you with a hundred other guys is not my favourite occupation.'

'No.' Julie forced the lingering regrets about her father's death to the back of her mind, and smiled. 'I think I know what that is.'

'Why not?' he demanded irrepressibly. 'You know everything else about me.'

Julie rested her head in the hollow of his shoulder. 'Your mother? Is she very formidable?'

Dan's chest heaved beneath her as he laughed. 'Not very,' he said reassuringly. 'Not where I'm concerned.'

'You are her only son.'

'And you're going to be her only daughter-in-law.'

'Am I?' Julie lifted her head and looked into his eyes. 'Am I really?'

'You'd better believe it,' he told her fiercely, and there was no better convincer than the urgency of his kiss.

Eight weeks later, Julie walked out of the limpid blue-green waters of the Caribbean, up the honey-pale sand to where her husband was reclining beneath a date palm. Dan had propped himself against the bole of the tree to pluck the strings of his guitar, but he put it aside as Julie approached him, stretching out his hand towards her and pulling her down beside him.

'Mmm, you taste salty,' he murmured, nuzzling her nape. 'But I must admit I like the flavour.'

Julie returned his kiss with feeling and then pressed him away from her. 'You'll get wet,' she teased, indicating his sweatshirt, but he only flopped back on to the sand, pulling her on top of him.

'I guess I can stand it,' he remarked lazily. 'Did you enjoy your swim?'

'Very much,' she agreed, and then pleased him by turning pink. 'Were you watching me?'

'All the time,' he told her huskily. 'I told you it was good. Perhaps I'll join you tomorrow.'

'Dan, if this wasn't a private beach——'

'—I wouldn't suggest it,' he grinned, and she hid her face in the hollow of his throat.

Later, after she had towelled herself dry and resumed the bikini she had shed before bathing, Dan stroked a rueful finger down her spine.

'Only four more days,' he said, with a sigh. 'I don't want to leave. I don't want to take you back and share you with the rest of my family.'

Julie smiled. 'Darling, we'll have our own home, our own house. We needn't go out a lot, if you don't want to.'

Dan pulled her close to him. 'At least Dad's promised me that job in Toronto in the spring. You'll like Toronto. It's not so abrasive as New York. And we'll have more time to ourselves.'

Julie shook her head. 'You may get tired of that . . .'

'Never,' he said vehemently. 'I can never get enough of you. You're under my skin, and in my blood. You're a delight and a temptation, and I can't believe you're my wife.'

'You'd better believe it,' said Julie humorously, glancing down at her still flat stomach. 'Remember, there'll be three of us moving to Toronto in the spring.'

'I know.' Dan's eyes were gentle, and his hands slid possessively over her stomach. 'Don't you really mind?'

'Do you?'

'Oh, honey . . .' His lips stroked her ear with warm insistence. 'I can think of nothing more desirable than knowing my child is growing inside you.' His eyes darkened into passion. 'You don't know how good that makes me feel.'

'I do,' she breathed unevenly. 'The child—he's ours. He's part of you, in me . . .'

Dan was not proof against such emotive talk, and for a while only the seabirds disturbed the deepening shadows of late afternoon. But at last he let her go, and Julie sat up, looping her arms around her drawn-up knees.

'Can we go and see Pam and David when we get back to New York?' she asked, gazing out towards the shadowy outline of Martinique, only twenty miles distant, and Dan stretched lazily.

'If you like,' he said drowsily. 'But be prepared for my mother to want to take care of you. You're going to have her first grandchild. She can be very possessive.'

'Like her son,' declared Julie provokingly, and then added: 'Do you think we could take Brad out in the yacht one evening? I once promised I would ask you, but I never did.'

'I guess so.' Dan grinned up at her. 'You know, perhaps we ought to stay with Anthea and Max. I got the feeling at the wedding that she admired you for what you did. And now that Corinne's decided to go to England ...'

Julie shrugged. 'If you like. So long as we're together.' She glanced down at him. 'I never knew one person could be so happy!'

Dan sat up, and draped a lazy arm about her shoulders. 'We're very lucky,' he agreed, kissing her shoulder. 'Now, shall we go back to the villa? Clothilde will be preparing dinner, and I want to take a shower first.' He paused before adding wickedly: 'With you.'

Later that evening they sat on the verandah of the villa, at peace with the muted sounds of the island. The Prescotts owned this villa at Cap d'Emeraude in St Lucia, and these past four weeks of their honeymoon had been a heavenly time of sun and sand and water, and warm, intoxicating nights of love. Already Julie had a kind of glow about her, that wasn't just the result of the golden tan she had acquired, and Dan's possessive gaze rested often on her lissom form. They loved, and they were in love, and they needed no one else.

Now, however, Julie sighed, and Dan, attuned to her every mood, leaned towards her perceptively.

'I know,' he said. 'You're feeling sorry for Price. I'm sorry you had to find out.'

'Your father knew I would want to know,' she said, touching his cheek with tender fingers. 'You were right to show me his letter. Things have been kept from me for too long.'

Dan nodded. 'Adam had it coming.'

'What will they do to him?'

'What can they do? He didn't actually cause your father to take his own life. The business over the debts may warrant investigation, but I doubt there's enough evidence to convict him.'

Julie shook her head. 'Would you think I was silly if I said I'm glad?'

'No.' Dan covered her fingers with his, and squeezed, and she went on:

'I—I have so much, somehow. I can't begrude him his freedom.'

'I wouldn't have you any other way,' said Dan huskily. 'Come on, let's go for a walk. We still have four more days —ninety-six more hours! And I intend to make the most of them ...'

Harlequin Presents...

The books that let you escape
into the wonderful world of romance!
Trips to exotic places...interesting
plots...meeting memorable people...
the excitement of love....These are
integral parts of Harlequin Presents—
the heartwarming novels read by
women everywhere.

Many early issues are now available.
Choose from this great selection!

Choose from this list of Harlequin Presents editions

Relive a great romance...
Harlequin Presents 1980
Complete and mail this coupon today!

Harlequin Reader Service

In U.S.A.
MPO Box 707
Niagara Falls, N.Y. 14302

In Canada
649 Ontario St.
Stratford, Ontario, N5A 6W2

Please send me the following Harlequin Presents novels. I am enclosing my check or money order for $1.50 for each novel ordered, plus 59¢ to cover postage and handling.

☐ 165	☐ 175	☐ 184
☐ 166	☐ 176	☐ 185
☐ 168	☐ 177	☐ 186
☐ 169	☐ 178	☐ 187
☐ 170	☐ 179	☐ 188
☐ 172	☐ 181	☐ 189
☐ 173	☐ 182	☐ 190
☐ 174	☐ 183	☐ 191

Number of novels checked @ $1.50 each = $_____

N.Y. State residents add appropriate sales tax $_____

Postage and handling $_____.59

TOTAL $_____

I enclose _____
(Please send check or money order. We cannot be responsible for cash sent through the mail.)

NAME _____
(Please Print)

ADDRESS _____

CITY _____

STATE/PROV. _____

ZIP/POSTAL CODE _____

Offer expires June 30, 1980.

00456406000

What readers say about Harlequin Presents

"I feel as if I am in a different world every
time I read a Harlequin."
A.T * Detroit Michigan

"Harlequins have been my passport to the
world. I have been many places without
ever leaving my doorstep."
P.Z. Belvedere Illinois

"I like Harlequin books because they tell
so much about other countries."
N.G. Rouyn. Quebec

"Your books offer a world of knowledge
about places and people."
L.J. New Orleans. Louisiana

"Your books turn my…life into something
quite exciting."
B.M. Baldwin Park. California

JOY
ROMANCE
LOVE

Harlequin Omnibus
THREE love stories in ONE beautiful volume

The joys of being in love...
the wonder of romance...
the happiness that true love brings...

Now yours in the HARLEQUIN OMNIBUS
edition every month wherever
paperbacks are sold.